W9-AUN-993

Ghost Girl

Ghost Girl

A Blue Ridge Mountain Story

Delia Ray

Thorndike Press • Waterville, Maine

Published in 2006 by arrangement with Clarion Kids, an imprint of Houghton Mifflin Company.

Thorndike Press® Large Print The Literacy Bridge.

The tree indicium is a trademark of Thorndike Press.

The text of this Large Print edition is unabridged.
Other aspects of the book may vary from the original edition.

Set in 16 pt. Plantin by Al Chase.

Printed in the United States on permanent paper.

Library of Congress Cataloging-in-Publication Data

Ray, Delia.
    Ghost girl : a Blue Ridge Mountain story / by Delia Ray.
        p. cm.
    Summary: Eleven-year-old April is delighted when President and Mrs. Hoover build a school near her Madison County, Virginia, home but her family's poverty, grief over the accidental death of her brother, and other problems may mean that April can never learn to read from the wonderful teacher, Miss Vest.
    ISBN 0-7862-8876-0 (lg. print : hc : alk. paper)
    1. Large type books.   [1. Schools — Fiction.
2. Teachers — Fiction.   3. Grief — Fiction.   4. Hoover, Herbert, 1874–1964 — Fiction.   5. Hoover, Lou Henry, 1874–1944 — Fiction.   6. Virginia — History — 20th century — Fiction.   7. Skyline Drive (Va.) — History — 20th century — Fiction.   8. Large type books.]   I. Title.
PZ7.R2101315Gh 2006
    [Fic]—dc22   2006014119

For Dad
a true mountain man in deed and spirit

Acknowledgments

■■■■■■■■■■■■■■■■■■■■■■■■■■■■

I would like to thank the staff at the Herbert Hoover Presidential Library in West Branch, Iowa, for patiently guiding me through their fascinating collection of Hoover letters, diaries, and photographs. I am grateful to George Nash for reviewing my manuscript and sharing his extensive knowledge about the Hoover family. During the initial stages of this project, Darwin Lambert and the staff at the Shenandoah National Park Archives provided valuable answers to my questions about the park's history. I also owe a great deal of thanks to the sons of Christine Vest Witcofski — Robert and Richard Witcofski — who so graciously provided details and information about their mother's life.

Thanks to my wonderful writing group — Terri Gullickson, Carolyn Lieberg, Jennifer Reinhardt, Julie Wasson, and Adeline Hooper Samuels — for generously giving your talents and support. And finally, thank you again to my faithful team of undercover editors — Matt, Caroline, Susanna, Lily

Howard, and especially Bobby Ray — for serving as a constant source of inspiration, encouragement, and writing wisdom.

1929

One

■ ■

'Course I never believed Dewey Jessup when he said he had met the president of the United States. Dewey was always telling tales about one thing or another — about his pa being the best preacher in the whole Blue Ridge. About how fast he could run, how far he could spit.

But there he was, standing like a hickory stump in my way, boasting about how he had just spent the afternoon with President Herbert Hoover, how he got to see every little hidey-hole of Camp Rapidan, the president's new summer place down the mountain.

"I brung him a baby possum for his birthday," Dewey told me.

I looked sideways at his dusty feet and worn-out overalls. "You brung the president a *possum?*"

"Yep," he said, poking his chest out. "Pa told me he heard it was Mr. Hoover's birthday and that he was at Camp Rapidan to go fishing. So I caught a little bitty possum hiding up under our shed. Then I throwed

11

him in a gunnysack, went right over there, and gave that possum to the president."

"What about all them marines they got watching the place?" I asked. "They just let you walk right past?"

Dewey was ready with his answer. "None of them marines even seen me," he bragged. "I snuck through the woods, round the back way. Pretty soon I was settin' on their settin' porch, with my feet up, eating on a big piece of layer cake."

"Huh," was all I said. I pushed by him. Mama wanted me to go fetch some snap beans from Aunt Birdy's garden and get back before dark, so I had to hurry. Night always came an hour early to our hollow over on Doubletop Mountain.

"Don't you want to know what-all me and the president talked about?" Dewey asked. He stuck right to me like a mayfly, but I never even turned my head.

"Miz Hoover asked where me and all the kids round here go to school. You should have seen her face when I said there weren't no school to go to. She turned just as white as your hair, April Sloane."

I kept marching straight up the trail, holding tight to Mama's best oak-split basket. Dewey and his friends were always teasing me about my towhead and my light eyes and my skinny arms. They called me ghost girl.

"Better watch out, ghost girl!" they'd holler. "We can see right through you!"

Dewey was still following, practically breathing down my back. "Miz Hoover says since we don't have a school, the president and her might just have to see about getting us one."

I stopped cold, then turned around real slow. "What did you say?" I asked.

A big grin spread out over Dewey's wide face. "I said, the Hoovers say they're gonna build us a school."

"You're lying again, Dewey Jessup," I whispered.

His grin turned sour. "That so?" He smirked at me and reached down into the pocket of his overalls. "If I'm lying, ghost girl, then where'd I get this?" He waved something green at me.

It was cash — a five-dollar bill. I had seen a five-dollar bill only a few times before — hiding down in Mama's money jar, when Daddy had steady work at the tannery.

I was already halfway to Aunt Birdy's place, and Dewey was still crowing. "Five dollars!" he hollered after me. "President Hoover give me five dollars for that little bitty possum!"

I first heard the hammers a couple months later when I was out hunting ginseng root. Kneeling there in the hickory shadows, in the finest patch of sang I had come across all October, I felt a chill run up my neck. A little voice breezed through my head. *"He weren't lying after all,"* it said. *"He weren't lying after all."*

Right away, I wanted to track down the pounding of those hammers and make sure it was true — that we were getting our very own school — but I knew Mama would be hot if I came home without my sang sack full. She was planning on drying the roots and fetching a good price for them down at Taggart's store. Folks with rheumatism would pay their last dime for a chance to brew the ginseng into tea and ease the ache in their joints. So I grabbed up my sang stick and went back to digging the spidery roots out of the ground, trying to push the echo of those hammers out of my head.

It wasn't until after we'd had a few hard frosts that I managed to get away from chores long enough to see for myself what was happening. I found the workers up on the ridge above Aunt Birdy's place. They had already laid down a layer of stone, and a frame of timbers was rising high up over it, higher than any cabin or barn I'd ever seen. I reckoned that if you stood on the roof you'd be able to see all the way over our rolling mountains — over Fork Mountain and Doubletop and Stony — maybe all the way to Criglersville.

I climbed a little closer and saw that Preacher Jessup, Dewey's pa, was there, working alongside the other men. Then, the next thing I knew, Dewey himself was coming up over the ridge, bringing his daddy supper in a tin pail. He was whistling, like always. And like always, I knew the tune right off.

Whistling was one of the reasons I despised Dewey Jessup. He didn't just whistle any old songs. They were *my* songs — ones that Mama and Daddy and Riley and I had listened to over and over on our Victrola.

I'll never forget the day when Daddy brought the Victrola home in the back of the wagon. At first Mama was angry when she heard he'd traded a month's work down in the valley for a phonograph. But when Daddy cranked the handle and the first notes of sweet music filled up our cabin, even Mama had to smile.

That was all before my little brother died and Mama made Daddy sell the Victrola and our stack of records to the Jessups because they reminded her of Riley and because we needed the extra money. Now that smooth red mahogany case with the turntable inside was sitting in Dewey's front room, and every day he walked around whistling the tunes that rightly belonged to me.

Before Dewey saw me, I scooted behind a pile of lumber and watched him through a chink in the boards. While the workmen sat down to eat their supper, he walked around the building two or three times with his chest pushed out farther than ever. I smiled to myself, thinking about what my Aunt Birdy would say — "just a backyard goose struttin' like a front-lawn peacock."

I was feeling antsy and getting ready to sneak out when I heard a low rumbling sound that made my stomach flip-flop. I peeked through the boards again, and pulling up in front of me was a shiny black automobile, long and sleek as a bull snake. The workmen were just as shocked as I was. They froze in the middle of chewing, with biscuits and drumsticks halfway up to their faces.

The car rolled to a stop, and a man in a black suit hopped out of the driver's seat. He hurried around to open up the back door, and then out stepped two city ladies bundled up in thick coats with fur collars. I could almost hear the squeak of Dewey's jaw dropping open.

One of the women marched right up to all those fellows staring and introduced herself as Miss Fesler, personal secretary to Lou Henry Hoover. She shook hands with a tall man, who said he was the building foreman, and then with Preacher Jessup. I was so anxious to hear what they were talking about, I almost forgot to stay hunkered down behind my woodpile.

"That's right," the woman was saying. She spoke fast, with a voice full of good manners. "We drove down from Washington just this morning. The first lady wanted me to check on the progress of the school and bring along one of our candidates for the teaching position here."

The other woman stepped forward to shake hands. "How do you do?" she said. "I'm Christine Vest." Preacher Jessup bobbed his head hello. I could see Dewey sliding closer, trying to get noticed.

"Mrs. Hoover wanted Miss Vest to come for a visit," the secretary went on, "so she could see what she might be getting into." She gave a tinkly little laugh. "She might head straight back home after the drive this morning. With the condition of these roads up here, sometimes those hundred miles from Washington seem more like a thousand."

Christine Vest. The sound of her name was so clean and crisp, I couldn't help whispering it back to myself. She was pretty, too, with big, soft deer eyes and wavy brown hair tucked up under a hat with a tiny red feather peeking out the side.

"We were hoping you could take us on a little tour of the building site," Mrs. Hoover's secretary said to the foreman. "I'd like to give Miss Vest a better idea of what the schoolhouse will look like once it's finished."

I strained to hear more, but soon they were drifting away and I could make out only snatches of talk about the classroom and electric lights and the adjoining teacher's quarters, about the finest this and the best of that. My legs were aching with cold and so much squatting. If it hadn't been for Dewey standing a stone's skip away, gawking at that long black car with the driver sitting inside, I would have tried to make a run for Aunt Birdy's.

But then I saw Miss Vest, the teacher lady, heading toward me, wandering over to take in the view. She stopped right alongside my lumber pile, close enough for me to hear her sigh when she looked out over the mountainside. When I calmed myself enough to peek out again, she was biting her lip and pulling her fur collar tighter around her neck. I saw her frown down at her high-heel shoes sinking into the red clay.

I wondered if what the secretary said was true, if Miss Vest might want to head straight home after seeing our mountains. I glanced over my shoulder at the valley, and all of a sudden I saw things the way she might be seeing them. Everything was winter-brown and lonely looking, especially with all the dead chestnut trees standing like skeletons below.

Before the blight came and started killing all the trees off, folks on the mountain used to pick up chestnuts by the bushel to sell down at Taggart's. Mama said when she was a little girl, she could earn enough money from the nuts to buy all her family's shoes plus sugar and coffee for the year. And like a lot of other men, Daddy worked at the tannery, where they used the acid from the chestnut bark to cure animal hides and turn them into leather.

But then the blight hit and the tannery closed down. Daddy had to start taking odd jobs to make ends meet. By the time I was old enough to go chestnut hunting, nuts were hard to come by and I was used to seeing whole forests of dying trees. Sometimes at night the mountain looked near haunted, with all those bare, towering trunks shining silver under the moon.

Pretty soon people started calling the chestnuts ghost trees, just like they took to calling me ghost girl right about the time my little brother, Riley, passed on. But I never used that name — ghost tree — myself. I knew there was life still hiding way down inside those old chestnut trees.

I was so sad and lost in thinking about the chestnuts and Riley and our old Victrola that I didn't even notice that Miss Vest had turned and was staring straight at me. My white hair must have caught her eye. She took a step closer and smiled. I stared back for a second, soaking up her sweet face. But then I saw Dewey coming, looking like he had just smelled something rotten.

So I tore out of there, with the shoestrings on my boots flapping, and I ran off down the mountain, leaving Dewey and Miss Christine Vest gazing after me.

Two

When I got home to Doubletop, Mama was standing out back at the battling bench, pounding dirt out of Daddy's overalls. Even with the cold bite in the air, I could see that her face was hot and shiny with all the pounding and standing over the steaming wash pot. "Shoot," I whispered to myself, knowing I was already in trouble. Ever since I turned eleven back in April, the washing had been left to me. But now Mama was near halfway through the basket of dirty clothes sitting at her feet.

Mama hardly looked up when I came running around the side of the cabin. Still, I could see her mouth tightening up into a hard little line — the same one that seemed to have been marking her face like a scar for the past year. I hurried back and forth, throwing more kindling into the fire under the big iron wash pot.

Pretty soon Mama hoisted Daddy's wet overalls into the pot. I grabbed up the paddle and gave them a stir in the boiling water and lye soap. "Where you been all morning?" she finally asked.

I was still trying to get my breath back from running so far. "I been up to where they're building the new schoolhouse, Mama," I said, panting. "And wait till you hear. There was two ladies up there from Washington, D.C. One of 'em might be the new teacher for President Hoover's school, if she decides to come. And you should have seen her, Mama. She was wearing stockings and high-heel shoes with a handbag to match and —"

Mama cut me off with her look, staring at me like I was addled. "What are you thinking about, April? You think when those Hoovers finish building that school-house that me and your daddy are just gonna let you traipse up there for lessons all day long?"

I was too surprised to answer. Mama sighed and wiped a lock of sweaty hair off her forehead with the back of her hand. "Just look at this place," she said. I watched her glancing round at the pile of dirty clothes, the chickens waiting to be fed, the door of the spring-house hanging off its hinges.

"You're the only help I got now," Mama went on in a sagging voice. "I can't be sending you off to spend all your time with some lady in stockings and high heels. So you best just clear that idea right out of your head." Then she wiped her hands on her apron and headed inside, letting the screen door bang shut behind her.

There was no use running after her trying to argue. Mama never listened. All I could do was swallow down my words and add a few tears to the water boiling away in the wash pot.

I ended up where I always did when some worry or another kept chewing at me. I ended up at Aunt Birdy's. As soon as she opened the door of her little clapboard house, I held out the stone I had been saving for her. She plucked it out of my hand, then raised it up to a streak of sunlight pouring through the tangle of old wisteria vines.

"I found it up at the falls," I told her.

Aunt Birdy's face crinkled into a smile. "Look a'there," she marveled. "Looks like one of them scairdy little brook trout that nobody can ever get their hands on."

"You think it's good enough for your porch railing, Aunt Birdy?"

"Well, let's see how she shines up," she said, and pulled her polishing rag and tin of beeswax from her sweater pocket. Even though a cold breeze was rustling through the vines, she stepped out on the porch and settled herself down in her old cane rocker.

While she worked on the fish stone, I walked up and down along the railing, gazing at her collection. Ever since she was a girl, Aunt Birdy had been collecting stones with wondrous shapes. She found them in streams like Mill Prong and Laurel Run, carved out by ages of running water. The first one she found worth keeping looked just like a crescent moon. Then came the egg in a nest, a little bitty footprint, and two perfect halves of a heart that fit together. And on and on. Lined up on Aunt Birdy's railing, all those shiny black rocks glowed like jewels in a bracelet. I must have worn a rut walking up and down that porch so many times, forever stopping to pick up my favorites and hold them in my hand.

I sat on the top step to watch Aunt Birdy for a while. She smiled and turned her head this way and that while she worked. You never would have guessed she was my Mama's mother. Her real name was Bertha Lockley, but everybody called her Aunt Birdy — Birdy, I think, because she was small-boned and quick as a sparrow, always hopping from one chore to the next. Folks said I had her eyes, but I wasn't so sure. Aunt Birdy's eyes were blue jay blue. Mine were mostly gray, like two shallow pans of water.

While we were sitting there, the sound of hammers started up again over the ridge. Aunt Birdy stopped rocking. Her tiny feet barely touched the ground. "I near forgot, Apry," she said all in a rush. "I been wanting to ask if you heard about the schoolhouse they're building up yonder."

I nodded, wishing I could cover up my ears to shut out that clanking.

A faraway look wandered across Aunt Birdy's face.

"Shame your Grandpap Lockley's not alive to see it. First the president of the United States moving next door and now us getting our own schoolhouse." She shook her head. "*Law!* . . . Preacher Jessup says the school will be ready come New Year's."

Then all at once Aunt Birdy fixed me with those sharp eyes of hers. "Aren't you excited about the new school, Apry?"

I swallowed hard, trying to push down the aching in my throat. "Mama don't want me going," I managed to say.

"Why's that?" Aunt Birdy asked. I didn't look at her, but I could hear her voice bristling up.

"She wants me home for chores."

"Did you tell her you could do your work

25

'fore school, then more when you get home?"

"No, ma'am."

"Well, why not, honey?"

I felt old suddenly, older than Aunt Birdy with her skin so brown and papery. It was all I could do to muster up words to try and tell how I'd been feeling. "I can't scrap with Mama now, Aunt Birdy," I finally said, sighing. "Least not since Riley died. She's too sad still. Even Daddy tries not to cross her."

Riley. It was the first time I had let my brother's name spill out in months. Mama wouldn't even let us mention him since the accident, and sometimes I could see why. Just saying his name made me miss him even more — his flop of yellow hair and the new batch of freckles across his nose every summer. His steady breathing next to me at night and the way he always tried to carry things that were way too heavy for him.

Maybe if I could have just remembered the good, happy times with my brother, it would have been all right, but I couldn't stop there. Whenever I thought of Riley, that night came washing over me. I kept seeing it — the flames climbing up the tail of his nightshirt, the surprised look on his face after I had shoved him to the floor and wrapped him round and round in a quilt to put out the fire.

"You better not, Apry," he had cried, his blue eyes round as glass buttons. *"That's Mama's best quilt."*

"Hush," I had scolded. *"You just hush and lie still."*

Aunt Birdy was watching me, shaking her head. "You still think you're to blame, don't you? You still think it never would have happened if you hadn't gone out to fetch more wood?"

I nodded, squenching my eyes tight to keep the tears in.

"Well, that ain't true, Apry Sloane," Aunt Birdy went on. "It weren't your fault. You only left for a minute! How were you supposed to know he'd go playing by that fire. We *all* thought he knew better than that . . . but the Lord works his mysteries, and sometimes there ain't nothing we can do but hold tight and ride along. And I'm sorry to say it, but your mama's not helping one bit with all of her grieving and keeping you shut up at home."

She sprang out of her rocker and came to stand beside me, so close that I could smell the wood smoke clinging to her old sweater with the calico patches. "Hold out your hand," she said. Then she set the fish stone in my palm. It was beautiful, gleaming with wax and still warm from her polishing.

"Now, you worry about finding a spot for that on my railing," she said with her eyes blazing, "and I'll worry about making sure you get up to that school."

I closed my fingers over the stone and thanked the Lord and all his mysteries for Aunt Birdy.

Three

Whenever I could slip away during the next few weeks, I rushed over to watch the schoolhouse going up. A giant old chestnut with peeling bark and gnarled roots had been left standing out front in the school-yard. Even though it was dying of blight, the workmen hadn't cut it down. Maybe it was plain too big or maybe they hadn't had the heart. Either way, I was glad the chestnut was still there. It was perfect for leaning against, and from the nest of tree roots I had a clear view of the workmen high up on the roof of the schoolhouse, setting the stone in the chimney and laying the shingles around it.

When I had too many chores or it was too bitter cold to sneak up to the school, I spent the day searching Mama's face for signs that she had talked to Aunt Birdy and changed her mind. But there were none, and opening day kept getting closer. The double doors on the front of the schoolhouse had a fresh coat of paint now, white as the new snow on the ground, and more and more kids from the hollows were starting to poke around the schoolyard.

Then Christmas Eve came. Daddy was down in the valley finishing a string of odd jobs, so Aunt Birdy invited Mama and me over for supper. *Now!* I kept thinking all the way through dinner. *Ask her now.* But still Aunt Birdy never said a word. After the brown-sugar ham, she served us thick slices of fried apple pie, then sat down to join us.

"Apples dried up good this year," she said, nodding to herself. "Almost taste fresh."

"Mmm-hmm," Mama said, but she stared off to the side of her plate like she wasn't even tasting the special food she was chewing.

With Christmas and all, I should have expected that Mama would be thinking of nothing but Riley. She hadn't brushed her hair smooth in days, just kept wrenching it back tight in a rubber band. Used to be that every Saturday night she would wash her long straight hair with store-bought soap, then brush it dry by the fire. Daddy would come home late at night from work and lift up a hank of her blond hair and just stand there, breathing in the clean smell of it until Mama noticed Riley and me watching. Then she would shoo Daddy away, trying not to laugh.

I squirmed in my seat. That was all hard to picture now, with nobody talking at Christmas Eve dinner and Mama staring at empty air with her mouth pulled down tight. Before long she was scraping her chair back. As she set to clearing dishes, I wanted to lay my head on the table, right in the middle of all the crumbs, and cry. It looked like I was never going to get past the old chestnut in the schoolyard.

Then I felt Aunt Birdy's shoe on top of my foot, gently pressing down. I stole a glance over at her, but she was eating her last bite of crust, smacking her lips like nothing had happened.

"You gonna help clear, April?" Mama asked.

"Yes, ma'am," I said, jumping to my feet.

Aunt Birdy set her fork on her plate with a loud clink. "Sit back down, you two," she said. "I want to ask you something."

Mama looked surprised, but she sat anyway and watched as her mother reached into her sweater pocket and brought out a grubby, folded piece of heavy paper. Aunt Birdy laid it on the table and smoothed out the creases one by one. I recognized it right away — it was the sign from Taggart's that had been taped up on the cash register for as long as I could remember.

Aunt Birdy held it up and pointed to the faded handwriting. "Tell me," she said in a firm voice. "What does this say?"

Mama leaned forward and squinted at the sign, then shook her head, looking impatient. "Why are you asking *me*, Mama? Where'd you get that, anyway?"

Aunt Birdy's old face turned sly. "Down at Taggart's. And I'll tell you what it says, 'cause I just asked Henry Taggart two days ago when I went down to buy more brown sugar. It says, 'ROUND BACK. PLEASE RING FOR SERVICE.' " Aunt Birdy tapped each word with her finger.

Mama stared with her mouth half open. *"So?"* she said.

"So," Aunt Birdy answered, her voice rising, "I've been going to that store for twenty years or more, and half the time Henry Taggart is nowhere in sight. He's out back counting his money or checking his stock or swigging liquor or whatever he does back in that shed of his, and I stand by the counter, nice as you please, waiting around like an old cart mule. For twenty years this sign's been staring me in the face, saying, 'ROUND . . . BACK . . . PLEASE . . . RING . . . FOR . . . SERVICE.' " She jabbed the words again with her finger.

"And I never even knew it," she went on.

"Never even saw the bell hiding in the middle of all those dusty papers he's got spread over the counter there. . . . If I'da known, I would have rung the devil out of that bell every chance I got."

"Can you tell me why you're bringing all this up now?" Mama asked.

That's when Aunt Birdy glanced over at me with her blue eyes glittering. " 'Cause I want better for Apry. If there's a sign up at Taggart's that says, 'Please Ring' or 'Two-headed Chickens for Sale,' I want her to be able to read it. And now she's got a chance. Any day now, the president's gonna be opening that school and —"

Mama snorted. She sat back hard in her chair and crossed her arms. "So that's what this is about. Did she put you up to this?"

"No," Aunt Birdy said. "I've been thinking of this on my own ever since I heard the hammers start up. It's a *school,* Alma, right up the mountain from us."

Mama shook her head. That's when I decided to slip out and fetch another bucket of wash water from the pump. I didn't want to be there when she said no, when poor Aunt Birdy was pushed into begging and pleading with her own daughter. So I dawdled outside. At the pump I could feel my wet fingers sticking to the cold metal handle, but still I kept pumping, letting the water splash over the sides of the bucket. Finally, Aunt Birdy came out on the porch and called for me.

When I stepped out of the shadows, she was waiting to meet me at the door, her face crinkling into a slow smile. "You're going to school," she whispered.

"What?" I said, pushing my way around her to make sure it was true.

Mama hardly looked up from the dishes. "If your chores fall off, you'll have to quit."

That was all she said, but it was enough.

On Christmas Day, Daddy didn't show up till noon, bringing me only a crumpled sack of lemon drops. He brought Mama a new sewing basket with five tiny spools of thread, a set of needles, and a thimble fastened underneath the lid. But when he set the basket into Mama's lap, she didn't do much more than mumble thank you. She had spent most of the morning in her rocker, staring into the fire.

For once, though, I didn't mind so much. I sucked the sugar off my lemon drops till they turned sour, and dreamed about going to school, trying to imagine myself walking straight through those big double doors with their shiny coat of new paint.

1930

Four

When opening day finally came, I was up at dawn, racing through the feeding and milking like I had hot coals in my boots. Aunt Birdy had loaned me Grandpap Lockley's old pocket watch so I could get to school on time, and Mama had even let the hem out of my Sunday dress. It was blue with a lace collar and little rose-shaped buttons down the front, and even though the sleeves were too short to cover the bony knobs on my wrists, I still felt almost stylish heading off for the first day of school.

"Preacher Jessup says school starts at nine o'clock sharp," Aunt Birdy had told me.

As I hiked along the frozen trail, I huddled in my sweater and kept my fists shoved down in the stretched pockets, pulling my hands out only long enough to flip open the case of Grandpap's watch and check the time on the yellowed dial. I wanted to be there a half-hour early. Maybe I could even get settled in my new desk before the other kids showed up, before Dewey came in whistling and calling me names.

I took a deep breath and scrambled up the last ridge, feeling my heart bumping against my ribs. Then I saw the schoolyard, and my heart bumped even harder.

There were people everywhere, mostly men in dark overcoats, with hats pulled down over their eyes. They were clumped around the schoolhouse steps, talking loud and laughing, their breath making puffs of smoke in the shivery air.

It was strange to see automobiles parked on the bare mountainside, turned every which way. More cars were pulling in, and I saw two marines in green uniforms splattered with mud trying to push another car out of the ditch. They yelled back and forth to each other, straining to be heard over the gunning engine.

I was standing near the edge of the clearing deciding what to do next when I noticed a woman with her children coming up the trail from Big Meadows. It was Mrs. Woodard and her three wild red-haired boys all dressed in their Sunday best. Mrs. Woodard was carrying her new baby girl wrapped in an old sheepskin saddle blanket.

All of a sudden, a few men in the crowd by the schoolhouse caught sight of the Woodards. The next thing I knew, the men were swooping down on them like hawks on a nest of baby field mice. *Who were they?* They were pushing too close and shouting questions. I could see Mrs. Woodard grab her baby tighter to her chest and the three boys edging back toward their ma, even though they weren't the type to turn scared.

Aunt Birdy would know what to do. I turned to head down the hill toward her place. But it was too late. One of the men looking out over the chestnuts and the foggy valley had already spotted me. He whistled to his partner, and before I could tell my legs to get moving, there they were, standing two steps away, wearing a pair of sugar-sweet smiles.

"Hi, there," said the first fellow. He had a round face, little round eyeglasses, and hair that was combed back flat and shiny against his head. I had never seen a man look so fancy. "Mind if we ask you a few questions?" he said.

I didn't answer. The two of them glanced at each other real quick. Then the taller one, with a cigarette dangling from his lip, spoke up. "You can get your picture in the *Evening Star*, sweetheart." He patted the black case hanging round his neck. "You'd like that, wouldn't you? What's your name, honey?"

"April," I told him. "April Sloane."

The swanky one pulled a little pad of

writing paper from inside his coat and scribbled something down. "How old are you, April? About nine?" I could hear his pen scratching and smell his spicy hair tonic drifting over. "This your first time going to school?"

"Eleven," was all I said. "I'm eleven." I could feel them both looking me over.

"What do you think about President Hoover building a school for all you children?" Mr. Swanky asked.

Before I had a chance to think of an answer, he said, "Have you ever met the Hoovers before?"

I shook my head.

"What'd you have for breakfast this morning, honey?"

I had never heard such a fool question, but I told them anyway. "Two ham biscuits with apple butter and milk."

They both looked sort of disappointed, but then Mr. Swanky's eyes landed on my feet and he seemed to spark up again. "So Miss April, why don't you smile real big now and let Hank here take your picture." Then he poked Hank with his elbow and mumbled something out of the side of his mouth, thinking I couldn't hear. But I did.

"Make sure you get a good shot of those shoes," he said.

I looked down at my boots, feeling my face turn hot. What was he staring at? They were just an old pair of Mama's. I had never thought much about them before. But now I could see they were just plain ugly, two sizes too big and full of cracks, like dried mud puddles. And my woolens had slipped down on one side, showing my frozen blue leg underneath.

"Look up at me, sweetheart!" Hank was hollering. "Up here at the camera."

"Come on, April," Mr. Swanky said. "Don't you want your picture in the paper?" His voice was turning mean, but I couldn't seem to lift up my head. I kept my eyes fixed on my boots and the frost on the ground underneath.

Then I heard another voice. "Excuse me, gentlemen," a woman said. "I'd like to get all the children inside now so that we can begin."

It was *her,* Miss Christine Vest, delivered to my side like a guardian angel. She put her arm around my shoulders and pulled me into her soft gray coat with the fur collar.

The man with the camera stepped forward. "Wait a minute, Miss Vest. We just wanted to get a quick shot of this young lady before she goes inside."

41

"Sorry, gentlemen," Miss Vest called over her shoulder. "Maybe we'll have time for more photographs later." Then she tightened her grip and started steering me toward the schoolhouse. "Now, don't worry," she said under her breath. "I'll get you through these reporters. Just keep walking."

As soon as we got closer, the men — reporters, she called them — began shouting questions. In the crowd, I could see more cameras, and I flinched at the flashes of light and the popping sounds they made as we pushed our way through. A marine hurried over to clear a path for us.

"Excuse us. . . . Pardon me," Miss Vest said over and over again. She smiled and nodded when the reporters called her name but paid no mind to their questions. Before long, we were through the double doors, standing in a little hallway filled with rows of coat hooks.

Miss Vest yanked the door shut behind us. *"Goodness,"* she said, sighing and pulling off her coat. "Now I know why the Hoovers decided to stay in Washington this week."

She helped me hang up my sweater, then stopped, giving me a sly look. "I'm just glad I caught up with you before those newspapermen had a chance to run you off down the mountain again."

I smiled back.

"So you *are* the one I saw hiding behind the lumber pile on my first visit here," she said. She smoothed her hand along the side of my head. "I thought so. I'd remember that hair anywhere."

I blushed, suddenly wanting to fade into the row of coats hanging on the wall. She probably thought I was some sort of freakish thing with my hair and eyelashes, so pale and washed-out looking.

"Where are my manners?" Miss Vest said. "I haven't even introduced myself properly. I'll be your new teacher, in case you were wondering. And I'll be living here at the schoolhouse. That door behind you leads right into my apartment."

I glanced over my shoulder at the door and nodded, pretending I didn't already know her name, that I hadn't been thinking about her moving into the schoolhouse for months.

I was still standing there gazing into her wide brown eyes when another door beside us burst open and I heard Miss Vest let out a little gasp.

"What on earth?" she yelped, and I followed her into what must have been the classroom. It looked like a lightning storm had hit. The electric lights were blinking on and off, and in every corner of the room there was some kind of commotion. Mrs. Woodard's baby was squalling and the Woodard boys were playing chase around the desks and a few other kids were drawing on the chalkboard while their parents gossiped in the corner.

Miss Vest hurried off. I saw her scoot across the room and catch little Alvin Hurt playing with the light switch. Like me, Alvin probably had never seen electric lights before except down at Taggart's. For a minute I stood in the doorway, not knowing what to do. Then I noticed Dewey and his older sister, Ida, standing nearby with three of the newspaper people gathered around them. Dewey was answering questions, beaming like a cat in the sun. You could have heard him all the way outside, bragging about his new shotgun and how he didn't really need to be at school, he had already taught himself to read.

One of the reporters was a lady wearing lipstick red enough to flag a train. I saw her smile and give something to Ida — a black enamel vanity case. Ida squealed when the lady leaned over and showed her how to snap it open. "Oh, thank you, Miss

Daniels!" she cried. "Look at that! It's got a little mirror and rouge inside. Can I really keep it?"

"Sure you can, honey," the lady said. Just then Ida looked up and caught me watching, but she didn't even smile or say hello. She twirled around and ran off to show her compact to Luella Hudgins and some other girls talking in the corner.

"Can I have your attention, please?" Miss Vest called from the front of the room. Through the crowd, I could see her standing by her desk, biting her lip as she waited for everyone to quiet down, but no one was listening. Dewey and the reporters went on grinning and talking. A few more kids and their parents filed in the door, and over by the woodstove Silas Hudgins spit a mouthful of tobacco juice into the coal bucket.

Miss Vest made an impatient face. Then she grabbed a wooden-handled bell on her desk and shook it. At first nobody paid attention to that, either, but then she shook it again — this time hard enough to set everyone's teeth to rattling. I almost laughed, thinking about Aunt Birdy and the bell at Taggart's.

The whole room got quiet as a graveyard. Even the Woodard baby stopped crying.

"Thank you," Miss Vest said, looking a little embarrassed. She set the bell gently back on her desk. Then she said, "I'd like to welcome you all to the President's Mountain School. We've all been waiting for this day for a very long time. . . ."

Miss Vest spoke with her hands. I'd never seen anyone talk that way before, sweeping their arms back and forth through the air to make a point. But Miss Vest made it look natural, with her sparkly bracelet and her long, graceful fingers. I was watching so close I barely heard what she was saying until she stopped moving long enough to glance at her wristwatch.

"It's after nine o'clock," she said, finishing her speech. "So I'm afraid we'll need to say goodbye to all our visitors and members of the press for now."

The Woodard brothers, Dewey and Ida, Luella, Alvin, and all the other kids started scrambling for the finest pick of desks. By the time I found a place, the only one left was over in the corner beside a tall, ornery boy named Poke McClure. I'd seen Poke smile only once in my life, a long time ago when he had caught Riley and me wandering on his property. He had chased us through the woods, chucking crab apples at our backs.

Most of the parents were shuffling toward the door now, but the newspaper people didn't show any signs of leaving. When I turned around in my seat to give them an evil eye, I saw the lady reporter waving her hand back and forth.

"Oh, Miss Vest," she called out. "Just a few more questions. What about the Hoovers? Didn't the president want to be here for opening day?"

Miss Vest shook her head. "The Hoovers didn't want to add to the confusion by coming up today. They plan on visiting a little later this spring, once the roads are a bit more passable and the children have settled into a good routine."

A few reporters sighed and huffed and set to complaining in the back of the room. Miss Vest acted like she didn't hear. She pushed a piece of her wavy brown hair behind one ear and straightened a tall jar of dried pussy willows on her desk.

But the lady reporter wasn't done yet. "We hear you'll be living right here at the schoolhouse. What about your living quarters? Are they comfortable?"

"Very," Miss Vest said, smiling. "The Hoovers have made wonderful arrangements for me. There's a sitting room with a fireplace and a modern kitchen and large bedroom — even a spare bedroom for guests upstairs."

"Do you think we might have a little tour later?" the lady asked with a flutter of her thick black eyelashes. She sounded almost flirty.

Miss Vest stopped for a second, considering, then said, "I suppose that could be arranged."

"Miss Vest!" someone else hollered from the doorway. I recognized the voice right off. It was Mr. Swanky again. "Can you tell us where you taught before coming to the Blue Ridge?"

Miss Vest's cheeks turned pink. "Well, this is my first official teaching position, but —"

"Your *first?*" he said, raising his eyebrows. "Aren't you concerned, Miss Vest? I mean, this being your very first assignment, and here you are living all alone on top of a mountain in the dead of winter, responsible for teaching twenty-two children who have never stepped foot in a school before. . . . I mean, do you really think you're ready for this?"

"Well . . ." Miss Vest said in her careful voice, "the president and first lady of the United States seem to think so."

Everybody in the room busted out

laughing. I could have cheered at the bush-whacked look on Mr. Swanky's face.

Before he could say anything else, Miss Vest called out, "Sergeant Jordan?" and like magic, a tall marine with a bristle-brush haircut appeared and started herding all the reporters toward the coatroom.

When the room was still again, Miss Vest let out a big breath of air. She looked up and down the rows, taking us all in, and we stared back. At that moment I reckoned everyone was thinking the exact same thing — that Miss Christine Vest was the smartest, bravest, most beautiful woman we had ever laid eyes on.

Five

The reporters kept coming. Day after day a new round of notebook scribblers tromped through the classroom, pestering Miss Vest with more questions and leaving their muddy tracks on the floor. There were other visitors, too — men in dark suits from the school board, prissy do-gooder ladies from down in the valley, all sorts of nosy people hoping to catch sight of the Hoovers.

Then one morning a group of girls from a school named St. Anne's Academy came to visit. They all wore matching dresses and had ribbons in their hair, and they stared and whispered a lot until a short, chubby woman they called "Headmistress" told them to "please remain silent while observing."

"We just wanted to see the wonderful things you're accomplishing here," the woman said to Miss Vest with a smile full of teeth. "And we've brought along some donated school supplies and clothing for the children. Would you like the girls to bring in the donations now?"

"Oh, no," Miss Vest said quickly. "Of course, we're extremely grateful for your donations, but it might be less disruptive for the class if you left the items on the porch when you go."

I felt the muscles in my jaw relax a little. Thank goodness Miss Vest had enough sense to know how ashamed we would be if we had to sit there and watch those rich girls pass out their hand-me-downs. Still, I couldn't help wondering what kind of clothes they had brought for us. Maybe there would be starched, white blouses like the ones they were wearing, and enough red satin hair ribbons for every girl in the class.

"How long were you planning on staying?" Miss Vest asked. I could see she was working to stay polite.

"Oh, not more than an hour or two," the headmistress answered. "We'll just stand back against the wall. Please continue on with your lessons. You just pretend we're not even here."

Miss Vest pressed her lips together like she was holding back a puff of steam. "All right," she finally managed to say. "We'll just finish up our phonics exercises and reading lesson, then we'll let you be on your way." She turned on her heel and walked back to the chalkboard.

"All right, children," Miss Vest began. "Let's pick up where we left off. Who wants to recite the alphabet today?"

No hands went up.

"No one? Well, then, let's recite together: *A . . B . . C . . .*"

With the girls in the back of the room watching, we did a fine job with the alphabet. Usually things were a lot worse. Nobody had learned to sit still yet. With all the wiggling and squirming going on, I sometimes felt as if I was in a room full of puppies. Whenever Miss Vest started to teach her lessons, the Woodard brothers scuffed their boots on the floor and let their eyes wander. Ida checked her face in her new compact five times a minute, and Alvin worked on the hole in his trousers till it was the size of a soup bowl. But the worst was Poke. All day long, he jiggled his long, skinny legs up and down under his desktop, till my own chair was shimmying back and forth across the floor.

"Very good," Miss Vest said when we got to *Z* without stopping. "Now, how about vowels. Luella?"

Luella was our prize student. She never made a mistake.

Next were letter sounds, and after a while we were doing so well Miss Vest made a game of it. She wrote a letter on the black-board and called somebody's name, and that person had to say, as quick as they could, what sound the letter made.

She wrote a *B* and called on Dewey.

"Buh," Dewey said.

She wrote a *L* and called on me.

"Luh," I said, glad to get my turn out of the way.

Ida made the sound for *N,* and Rainey Walker managed to remember both sounds for the tricky *G.*

We were answering faster and faster and Miss Vest was smiling. Then she wrote *W* on the board and called out, "Poke!"

At first he didn't answer. Then he said, "Duh."

I knew why he said "Duh." Because of double-*U.* "Duh" for double-*U.*

But all of a sudden, we heard a snicker behind us. Then two or three more of the St. Anne's girls started giggling. Miss Vest looked mad enough to spit.

"Girls!" the headmistress lady snapped. "Quiet, please!"

But it was too late. A dark shade of red was already creeping up Poke's neck, past his big Adam's apple, up to the roots of his tangled black hair. He stared down at the top of his desk.

I was surprised. I didn't think the day would ever come when I felt sorry for Poke McClure. I turned around and glared at the line of girls leaning against the back wall. One of them still had a smirk playing along the corners of her mouth. The words were on the tip of my tongue. "Go back to where you came from," I was aching to say. "I wouldn't wear your old castoffs if you paid me."

I wasn't the only one who refused to go near the boxes of hand-me-downs. Nobody wanted to touch those clothes after the St. Anne's girls had laughed at us. And not long after their visit, the marines set up sawhorses at the bottom of the schoolhouse road and started turning all the reporters and other callers away. I was tickled. Maybe now I'd be able to learn something without a bunch of busybodies looking over my shoulder.

But we hadn't heard the last of the reporters. One morning Sergeant Jordan showed up with a fat brown envelope from the White House filled with newspaper stories about the President's Mountain School. Even though it was time for penmanship, Miss Vest loosened up on the rules for once. She passed around the stack of clippings and let everybody laugh and talk and take turns squinting at the photographs and the long rows of tiny print.

"Hey, there's me again!" Dewey kept shouting. It was true. Almost every article showed a picture of Dewey, standing by the blackboard, lounging on the schoolhouse steps, him and Ida walking home with big grins on their faces.

"You're famous, Dewey," Miss Vest said as she glanced over some of the clippings. "The *Washington Post*, the *Evening Star*, the *New York World.* Did you know they're calling you possum boy?"

"Yep," Dewey said proudly. "On account of me giving President Hoover that baby possum for his birthday. That's when he and Miz Hoover got the idea to build our school." He looked around to see who was listening.

Beside me, Poke made a disgusted noise in his throat. We had all heard that story fifty times already. And everybody had seen the reporters slipping Dewey change, even dollar bills, as he fed them more and more of his tall tales for their newspapers. I had overheard Ida telling her friends that Dewey had saved up enough money to buy himself a new suit of clothes at Taggart's.

When the pile of clippings finally came

around to me, I flipped through the stack as quick as I could, scared of seeing a picture of my ugly boots spread across a whole page. But luckily, I showed up in only one photograph. We were all sitting at our desks in the picture. I looked scrawny, with my mouth hanging half-open and my hair a white blur around my head. I had to stop myself from reaching down and smudging out my face with my finger.

Just then Miss Vest announced that it was time for penmanship.

"Oh, come on, Miss Vest," Dewey begged. "Can't you read some of the newspapers out loud? Please? So we can see what they're saying about us?"

"Not now, Dewey," she told him, gathering the clippings back into a stack. "We're already way behind on our lessons this week. I'll tack the articles up on the bulletin board later so that you can all look at them more this afternoon."

Everybody sighed, and we pulled sheets of paper out of our desks.

Penmanship meant we had to copy long rows of letters and rhyming words from the blackboard. Miss Vest read the words out loud: *bat, hat, cat, bed, fed, red.* But as usual, whenever I started writing, the letters seemed to swim together, and my hand felt sweaty and cramped holding on to my pencil.

When I first started school, I thought reading might come fast and all at once like a streak of lightning. But now a month or more had already gone by, and still no lightning bolt had hit. As soon as I got home every afternoon, Mama asked to see my work. She wasn't too impressed with my pages full of letters and crayon drawings. "When are you gonna start reading books?" she wanted to know. "Soon," I kept saying.

I could never tell her that the letters just didn't make sense, that all the blackboard exercises made me feel itchy and restless, like my whole body was covered in poison ivy blisters.

Poke must have been feeling the same way. During penmanship, he stared out the window, jiggling his legs like always. I sneaked a look over at his paper. He had copied only one row of letters from the blackboard so far, and his writing looked even worse than mine, all running downhill and smeared with pencil lead.

Miss Vest was watching Poke, too.

"Poke, are you having trouble with this assignment?" she asked.

"No," he muttered, hunching over his paper.

Miss Vest started to walk toward us. Poke wouldn't look up at her. Instead, he kept filling in a big O on his paper, making the circle black and angry looking, until all of a sudden, his pencil point snapped.

"Can I help?" Miss Vest asked quietly.

"I *said* no," Poke hissed, keeping his teeth clenched. Then he flung his pencil down and slouched back in his chair, crossing his arms over his chest.

Miss Vest tried not to flinch. She stood over him for a minute, staring down at the top of his head without saying a word. When he still wouldn't look up at her, she started back to her desk. I heard her sigh as she walked away. The truth was, nobody seemed to be paying much attention to the assignment. Luella had borrowed Ida's compact to paint two red spots of rouge on her cheeks, and up front some little kids were whispering and poking each other in the ribs.

Then Dewey spoke up. "Most of us are done, Miss Vest. Recess ain't for another ten minutes. Don't we have time for some of those newspaper stories now?"

At first I thought Miss Vest was getting ready to lose her temper. She swiped a mussed piece of hair behind her ear and stared at Dewey hard, but then she said, "As a matter of fact, I think we *do* have some time." Everybody looked up from what they were doing. Her voice sounded funny, too high and too cheerful.

"Maybe hearing what those reporters have to say about us is just what we need right now." She grabbed up the stack of clippings and started shuffling through them. "Let's see. . . . Here's one called 'Clans of Hillbilly Folk Welcome Book Learning in Hoover's Dark Hollow.' Or what about 'Wild Young Mountaineers Swarm to Hoover School'?"

She glanced up at us. Her face was flushed and her dark eyes glittered. "Not that one?" she asked, pretending to be surprised. "Well, how about this one from the *Washington Herald*?"

She cleared her throat and began to read: "Deep in the Blue Ridge Mountains, where snow now sifts through the wild oak branches, President Hoover's trim little school for mountain children opened its doors to more than twenty education-starved people last Monday. The First Lady will find ample outlet for her well-known humanitarian sympathies in the ragged little mountain children who have trooped from their mud-chinked log cabins scattered through the wooded depressions of the hills.

Some of these sad little wraiths are as shy as wild rabbits. They have never ridden on trains. Some have never even seen one. The biggest excitement in their lives has been 'hog-killin' time' at their mountain homes —"

"Hog-killing time?" Ida cried. "They think I like *hog killing?*"

But Miss Vest barely took a breath. She flipped through the stack and found another article to read, and then another. Why wouldn't she stop? The newspapers were all the same. All of them made us sound ignorant in one way or another, more like dumb farm animals than just regular folks without much money or nice clothes.

Finally, Miss Vest finished reading. She sat back on her desk with her shoulders drooped like all the life had just run out of her body.

"They're wrong," Ida shouted. "They didn't get nothing about us right."

"I know, Ida," Miss Vest said in a tired voice. "I'm sorry."

"Sorry?" somebody called out.

It was Poke. I jumped at the sound of his voice. Like me, he had barely said a word since school started, but now he was talking faster than ever, spitting out words like he was trying to get rid of a sour taste in his mouth. "You must think we're just a bunch of hillbillies, too," he said. "Must be why you keep giving us all these fool exercises. How you reckon we're gonna learn real reading and writing, copying them baby words off the blackboard all day long?"

Miss Vest looked shocked. "Poke, *of course* I don't agree with those reporters. I hate what they wrote. The only reason I read those silly articles out loud was to get your attention . . . everybody's attention."

She took a deep breath and went on, using her hands to talk again. She hit the air with her fists. "I *know* we can prove all those reporters wrong. But it takes work, and we all have to start with the basics. It wouldn't matter if I was teaching in the Blue Ridge or New York City, I'd still use the same methods to teach you. Learning to read and write takes time and patience and —"

"Well, I don't have that much time," Poke cut in, his jaw muscles working. "I reckon my pa would sooner have me home clearing stumps than sitting here making this hen scratch." He glared down at the paper on his desk with an evil look. Then before we knew it, he had shoved himself out of his desk and started scuffing up the aisle.

"Wait, Poke!" Miss Vest called out, her

voice sounding panicky.

But he was already out the door. Miss Vest dropped her hands to her sides. "Don't worry," she said softly, almost like she was trying to comfort herself. "He'll be back tomorrow."

But the rest of us knew better. Poke was gone for good.

Six

I was leaning against my chestnut tree at the beginning of recess a few days later when Dewey started whistling again. It was that same song he always whistled — "Let Me Call You Sweetheart" — and as he started the tune over and over, I could almost hear the man's voice from our old record, singing the words so waltzy and slow.

Dewey was pitching a baseball back and forth with Vernon Woodard. Every time the ball smacked his stiff leather glove, his whistling seemed to get louder. For a while I huddled down into my sweater, trying to block out the cold wind and the mournful sound of Dewey's high-pitched tune.

If they had given me half a chance, I would have joined Ida and Luella and the other girls sitting on the porch steps. They were bunched together looking at the new Sears, Roebuck mail-order catalog. Ever since Ida had spotted it on Miss Vest's desk the week before, she and her friends had met at recess every day to flip through the pages and *ooh* and *aah* over all the fancy things for sale.

Finally, I couldn't stand it anymore.

"Stop it, Dewey!" I yelled.

It seemed as though everybody in the schoolyard turned at once to look at me. Even the girls on the porch tore their eyes away from the catalog to stare.

"Stop what?" Dewey asked with a smirk.

"That whistling," I said, trying to keep my voice down. "You've whistled that song four times through already."

Dewey looked confused for a second, then his eyes lit up. He walked toward me, tossing the ball up and catching it in his glove. "I know why you want me to quit," he said with a sly smile creeping across his face. "I'm singing one of your old records. You're just sore 'cause *we* got the Victrola now instead of you. . . . Well, too bad, ghost girl, you better get used to it."

Then he started singing the words to the song in a loud, mocking voice. "Let me call you sweetheart, I'm in love with you. Let me . . ."

I closed my eyes. "Stop, Dewey," I said.

But he kept singing, and I could hear my voice getting louder and turning shrill. I clamped my hands over my ears and the next thing I knew I was screaming, "Stop! Stop! *I said stop it!*"

When I opened my eyes again, Dewey was staring at me like I had sprouted horns.

He opened his mouth to say something, but I didn't wait to hear. I started running for the schoolhouse, pushing past all the kids, who stood frozen, gawking at me.

The girls on the porch barely scooted out of the way as I raced up the steps.

"What's wrong with *ghost girl?*" I heard one of them say behind me.

When I burst into the classroom, Miss Vest was at her desk, looking over her lesson book.

"What's wrong, April?" she asked, springing up from her seat. She ran over and put her hand on my cheek. "You're shaking!"

"No, it's just —" I gulped for breath and swallowed down the quiver in my voice. "It's just a little cold out there, that's all. I just came in for a minute to get warm."

"Poor thing . . . Come stand by the stove. Maybe we should see about getting you a good winter coat and some warm shoes. Even though spring's around the corner, we've still got plenty of chilly days left." Miss Vest bustled about for a while, dragging a chair closer to the stove for me and putting more coal on the fire. She draped her sweater over my shoulders, and I hugged the sleeves around me, breathing in the smell of paste and chalk dust in the quiet classroom.

"Actually, I'm glad you came in early," she said after a few minutes. "I was just getting ready to start a project in the kitchen. Want to help me?"

I nodded and hung her sweater on the back of the chair, then followed her toward the door in the far corner of the classroom. *The door to the kitchen.* I had been itching to peek into Miss Vest's apartment ever since school started, especially when I heard Dewey and Ida carrying on about what it was like inside. Supposedly, Miss Vest had invited their whole family to come over one evening and listen to the radio. The next day, Ida had spent half a recess telling everybody what a fine time they had had — about Chubby Parker singing on the radio show and the spotless linoleum in Miss Vest's kitchen and the cookstove with four burners and the Frigidaire with the little ice chest inside.

Now that I was finally seeing the kitchen for myself, I just had to stand there blinking. I had never laid eyes on such a stretch of gleaming white. The counters were smooth and shiny and there were rows of creamy-painted cabinets with little cut-glass knobs and blue-and-white gingham curtains hanging in the windows.

Miss Vest closed the door behind her. Then she turned to me and said, "Tell me, April, have you ever had hot cocoa?"

I shook my head, trying to keep my mouth from hanging open.

Miss Vest's eyes were shining. "Well, we're going to make some right now," she said. "For the entire class." She rushed over to one of the cabinets and pulled the door open. I stared at the shelves full of food, all lined up neat as a pin in colorful tins and boxes. I was used to seeing food come home in plain white flour sacks or brown paper bags — never with fancy pictures and writing across the sides.

"Now . . . we'll need cocoa and sugar," Miss Vest said, choosing a few things from the shelves. "And lucky for us, Sergeant Jordan delivered some fresh milk this morning."

She hurried to the Frigidaire, and I took a couple steps closer, waiting to see what was inside. When she yanked open the door, a little light came on and a rush of air, cold as winter, hit me in the face. "Lordy," I whispered before I could stop myself. Miss Vest pulled out two big glass jugs of milk, pretending like she hadn't heard me. She pushed the door closed with her hip.

Then I saw her sneak a quick look at my hands. "Why don't we wash up a little before we get started?" she said. I looked down. My hands were grubby, all right. I always tried to clean up after chores every morning, but the light was so dim in our cabin, sometimes I got to school before I noticed ground feed corn under my fingernails or mud on the hem of my dress.

Miss Vest showed me to a deep sink underneath the kitchen window. Then she turned the silvery knobs and the faucet started spurting water. She laughed when I jumped back. "It's a lot easier than the hand pump outside, isn't it? Here . . . See if that temperature is all right."

I crept my hands under the water and held them there. "It's *warm,*" I said.

"That's right." Miss Vest reached for a cake of soap by the sink. "We have a tank that heats up the water for washing."

She held the soap out for me and I took it careful as I could. It didn't feel coarse like the lye soap Mama and Aunt Birdy made out of cow fat. And it smelled a sight better, too — like a whole basketful of rosebuds. But the best part of all was the bubbles, handfuls of them shining in the sunlight streaming through the window.

All of a sudden, the soap shot out of my hand. I chased it around the slippery sink for a while until I finally grabbed hold of it, but then it shot away again. That's when I found myself laughing — giggling, really. And the laughing kept coming up and getting bigger, just like the soap bubbles in my hands.

It felt so good. I could barely remember the last time I had been that tickled. It was probably the summer before Riley died, when we used to run away from Mama and her long list of chores and head up for Big Meadows. We'd stretch out on our backs in the grass, with Riley using my stomach for a pillow. Pretty soon he'd say some silly thing to get me going, then he'd start giggling at the way my laughing made his head bounce up and down on my stomach. And that was it. The harder he bounced, the more we laughed, until we were so wore out, we'd have to roll over and take a nap right there in the tall grass.

"April? What are you thinking?"

When I looked up, Miss Vest was staring as if she didn't know what to make of me. She handed me a soft towel to dry my hands, and all at once I felt the color rush to my cheeks.

"Oh, just about my little brother,

Riley," I managed to say.

Her eyebrows shot up. "I didn't know you had a little brother."

"Oh — I mean, I don't. He's dead now. . . . He died a while ago."

Miss Vest made a sad sound in her throat and I could tell she was getting ready to ask me more questions, so I turned away, searching for something else to look at. My eyes landed on a small picture in a gold frame on the windowsill.

"Who are they?" I blurted out.

"My mother and father back in Kentucky," Miss Vest said in a quiet voice.

"Kentucky?" I asked. "But I thought you were from Washington, D.C. Where the Hoovers live."

"Oh, no," she said proudly. "I was born and raised in the green hills of Casey County, Kentucky."

I leaned forward over the sink, peering closer at the photograph. I couldn't help being surprised. Miss Vest's mother and father were plain-looking folks, standing in front of a wagon of some sort, the woman wearing an apron over her long dress and the man in baggy overalls. Their smiles were bashful. Truth to tell, they didn't look much different from folks I was used to seeing every day.

Miss Vest picked up the photograph. "This was taken a few years ago during harvest time. See . . . you can just make out the tobacco leaves in the wagon behind them. Daddy had a good crop that year."

"Your daddy was a *farmer?*" I asked.

Miss Vest nodded. "Mmm-hmm. Still is," she said. "He's getting a little stiff in the joints these days, but somehow he makes it out to the fields every morning." She gazed down at the picture, her face turning softer. "He wrote me a letter this past summer, saying that he wished he still had me around to pull budworms off his tobacco stalks." She smiled, wrinkling up her nose.

Now I was the one staring, trying to picture Miss Vest as a young girl, moving up and down dusty tobacco rows, plucking at mushy old worms. Who would have ever believed it? Miss Vest, with her fine voice and swirly skirts and graceful hands.

"There was a time," she went on, "when I couldn't wait to leave Casey County. I promised myself that I would leave and never look back." She shook her head in wonder. "But here I am . . . right back in a place not too much different from where I grew up."

"Are you sorry?" I asked. The room was so quiet I could hear the shiny metal clock ticking on the wall.

"No," Miss Vest finally said. "It's just that — just that now that I'm here, I expected to have more answers."

She let her eyes roam around the kitchen, and for a minute she seemed to forget I was even there. I watched the worry flitting back and forth across her face like shadows. "I spent years going to a one-room schoolhouse a lot less fancy than this one," she said. "I went to school back in the hills. . . . I should know how to do a better job of teaching all of you — of teaching older boys like Poke without humiliating them — but that's something they really don't prepare you for in teachers' college. And now Poke's gone. I missed my chance to help him."

Miss Vest stared out the window over the sink as if she could see down into the hollow where Poke had disappeared. If I had had enough nerve, I would have told her. It wasn't *all* her fault. Poke's daddy spent most of the day drinking, and if the McClures wanted to eat, it was Poke who had to do most of the plowing and planting. With spring coming, he didn't have time to be patient with all those letter exercises. He had to learn *now,* so the next time he went down to Taggart's he could add up his own figures and sign his name on the credit slip.

Miss Vest gave herself a little shake. "I'm sorry, April." She sighed. "I don't know why I'm rattling on like this. I've just been worried about losing more students, I guess." Then she looked me straight in the eye. "*You're* not going anywhere, are you?"

Mama's tired face, all her questions about when I would start reading, flashed into my head. But I couldn't tell Miss Vest those things. "I'm not going anywhere," I told her, trying to sound sure of myself.

"Gracious!" Miss Vest cried all at once. "Look at the time, April! We better get this hot chocolate going before everyone comes in here after us."

So we went to work. Miss Vest showed me how to measure cocoa, sugar, and milk into a big pot on the stove. Then I stirred with a wooden spoon while she lined up rows of tin cups on two big trays. When we were done pouring the cocoa, Miss Vest reached up into the cabinet and brought out something wrapped in waxed paper.

"The most important ingredient of all," she announced, reaching up into the cabinet again and tossing more bags onto the counter, one by one. "*Marshmallows!* We've got a whole year's supply courtesy of Mr. Jeremiah Hickock, owner of the Hickock Confection Company. He wanted to send something special to President Hoover's school."

"What're *marshmellas?*" I asked.

Miss Vest ripped open a bag and handed me one. "Here . . . go ahead and try it." But I was too shy to taste it in front of her, so I smelled it instead, grinning over how it puffed back into shape when I squeezed it between my fingers.

Miss Vest smiled and glanced at the clock again. "How about if you put one of those in each cup while I go and bring everyone inside."

I nodded. When she was gone, I looked around, just to be sure no one was spying through the kitchen window, then I stuffed a whole marshmallow into my mouth. Then another and another. It was like eating clouds right out of the sky, clouds made of spun sugar. I could have sat in that bright white kitchen forever, tasting marshmallows, dreaming of Miss Vest as a girl, maybe just my age, working up and down the dusty tobacco rows.

Seven

The first Saturday in April, I woke up feeling happy. The sun had finally found its way to our hollow, melting the last dirty patches of snow and filling the air with the smell of the mountain turning green again. And Daddy was home for a change. He had finished his logging job down in the valley and had a few days off before it would be time to look for more work.

He was splitting wood out back when I woke up that morning. I hurried through my breakfast and washing dishes so I could help him.

"Happy birthday, Apry," Daddy said when he saw me coming.

I let out a little laugh. "I won't be twelve for another week, Daddy."

"I know. That's why I'm telling you now. I might be off on another job next week. . . . Come over here. I want to show you something."

Daddy led me around behind the woodpile to a little boggy place in the trees. He stopped under one tree and gently pushed at a clump of damp leaves with the toe of his boot. I smiled. Curling up from the dark earth was a perfect white blossom. I could have sworn I saw it trembling on its pale green stem.

"Lady's slipper," I breathed.

Daddy nodded. "First one I've seen this year. I always know it's time for your birthday when the lady's slippers come out." He shook his head, still studying the flower. "That's one thing your Mama and me always had in common. Our favorite month. April."

Daddy peeked at me with a little sideways grin. I waited for him to fall silent again, like usual. Most times, he was quiet as a cave. But he kept talking, and I leaned against him, letting his slow, deep voice rumble over me. "Some people call those moccasin flowers," he told me. "There's a story I remember hearing about a little Indian girl who wandered off in the snow. She wasn't wearing any shoes and it was bitter cold, and pretty soon night came along. The whole village went out hunting for her, but they never found her. The only trace they found was in the spring — a flower no one had ever set eyes on before blooming right in the spot where that little Indian girl was last seen."

I looked up at Daddy. "You think that's true?"

He shrugged. "Makes a good story for your birthday, don't it? Now you owe me some time at the woodpile."

I laughed and followed Daddy back to the chopping block. We spent the rest of the morning together, splitting wood and loading up the wagon with extra kindling for Aunt Birdy. After lunch we hitched up Old Dean and were just about to set off for Aunt Birdy's when Mama ran out on the porch.

"I wouldn't mind going with you," she called, pulling on her sweater.

Daddy couldn't hide the surprise in his voice. "That's fine," he said. "Climb on up." I scooted off the buckboard and settled in the back of the wagon, in the middle of the split logs, where I could get a good view of Mama and Daddy up next to each other. I hadn't seen them sitting side by side for months, and as we started off, I almost felt like humming. Springtime coming had brought out the best in all of us, even Old Dean. His step was lively and his nostrils flared in and out, taking in the fresh piney-wood smells.

Daddy was quiet again, but a few times I saw him turn his face up to the sun coming through the trees. He let the reins go loose in his hands, leaving Old Dean to find his own way down the trail. Mama was livelier, too. She even started pointing things out along the way. "Listen to them blue jays courting," she said. Then, a little farther along, I heard her say, "Look a'there. Lady's slippers!" We all turned to stare for as long as we could at a patch of white blossoms growing in a gully beside the trail. Mama's gray eyes didn't look quite so tired, and the sharp air had brought out some color in her cheeks. Daddy winked at me over his shoulder.

By the time we pulled into Aunt Birdy's clearing, it had warmed up enough to take our sweaters off. I jumped down from the wagon and ran ahead to check whether Aunt Birdy had any new stones on her railing. There weren't any, but the view from the porch was fine. The valley almost glowed with the bright green haze of new leaves budding on the trees.

Mama stopped to admire the view. Then she clumped up the steps and knocked once on the door.

"Ma?" she called, pushing the door open. "We got a load of wood for —" Her voice broke off, and then I heard her say, "Oh. Didn't know you had a visitor."

I peeked in to see who it was, and there in

Aunt Birdy's front room was Miss Vest, settled into a cane rocker by the fire.

"Well, hello there, April," she said with a big smile.

Aunt Birdy hopped up from her chair to greet us. "Ain't this a surprise? April's schoolteacher coming by to call, and now you all here! Come on inside!"

Miss Vest stood as we shut the door behind us and reached out her hand to Mama. "It's a pleasure to meet you, Mrs. Sloane. I've been hoping we'd have the chance to meet soon. You have a fine daughter here." Miss Vest glanced at me and I felt silly, knowing my mouth was stretched into a fool grin, ready to split my face in two.

Aunt Birdy was beaming, too, but when I looked at Mama, she wasn't smiling at all, and it took her a long time to notice Miss Vest's hand hanging in the air. She finally gave it a clumsy little shake.

"Alma Sloane," she said in a flat voice. "This here's my husband, Wesley."

I could see Mama looking Miss Vest up and down, taking in her hairstyle, her plaid wool skirt and soft blue sweater with the pearly buttons. Mama started tucking the limp strands of her own hair behind her ears and smoothing her homely cotton dress over her middle, and all of a sudden I felt ashamed for her and mad, too. She had been acting happy on the ride over. Why couldn't she smile now? Why couldn't she just take my teacher's hand and say "Pleased to meet you" and "How's April doing in school?"

Miss Vest started chattering, trying to make up for the sudden quiet in the room. "I've been out calling on some of my students' families today," she said. "I actually thought of trying to find your place, but I was afraid of getting lost."

Daddy nodded. "Yes, ma'am," he said. "Best to know your way if you're heading over to Doubletop."

"I was on my way home when I noticed Aunt Birdy on her porch," Miss Vest said. "I thought I better stop in and say hello since she's my nearest neighbor. Then I found out she was your grandmother, April. . . . I meant to stay ten minutes, but I've been here more than an hour." Miss Vest gazed around the room, shaking her head. "It's like walking into a curiosity shop," she said.

I had never heard of a curiosity shop before, but somehow I knew what Miss Vest meant. You could spend all day in Aunt Birdy's front room and still discover something new the next time you came. Every spare inch of shelf and windowsill was covered with geegaws. There were things you might expect lined up on planks around the fireplace, like baskets of mending and canning jars full of pickled green tomatoes and peaches. But jumbled in were Aunt Birdy's keepsakes — more of her best river stones, the reddest cardinal feather and knobbiest turtle shell you ever saw, and little carvings of chestnut wood that Grandpap Lockley had whittled when he was a boy. Even the ceiling was busy, hung with bunches of dried herbs and roots for brewing into medicinals.

Mama was running out of patience. "Well, Wes," she said, folding her arms across her chest, "we better get to unloading that wood 'fore it gets too late in the day."

Miss Vest touched her arm. "Oh, just a minute, Mrs. Sloane. Would you mind if I showed you one thing first?" She hurried over to a leather satchel she had left by the rocking chair, reached inside, and hefted out a big book. It was the Sears, Roebuck mail-order catalog.

"During my calls this week, I've been asking all the parents about an order we'll be sending off soon to Sears, Roebuck," Miss Vest explained. "A lot of the students need new school shoes, and when I went down to Taggart's the other day, I realized Mr. Taggart only stocks a few styles and not very many sizes for children."

Then she stopped, glancing down at my old boots. "Now that you're here, I thought I could get April's shoe size, if you like, and send the order off on Monday morning."

Aunt Birdy scurried over, lighting on the catalog like a fly on jam. "Mind if I look at that for just a minute, miss?" she asked, and without waiting for an answer, she took the catalog out of Miss Vest's hands, then sat herself down in the rocker and started rustling through the pages.

I felt Mama stiffen up beside me. "April's boots still got plenty of wear left in 'em," she said. "And besides, we ain't put away any money for Sears, Roebuck school shoes. I reckon they don't come cheap."

"Oh, there's no need to worry about that," Miss Vest said quickly. "The Hoovers have set up a fund for those sorts of things. They knew that the children would be walking a long way to school and would need extras, like sturdy shoes and warm mittens."

"No, thank you, just the same," Mama said, her voice turning hard.

Aunt Birdy looked up from the catalog, and the room got still again until Daddy finally cleared his throat. "Ain't no harm in it, Alma," he said. "Long as all the others are getting 'em."

"Look here, Alma," Aunt Birdy said, poking her finger at a page in the catalog. "Here's some pictures showing which ones Apry could —"

Mama cut her off. "No use me arguing," she said. "Seems like everybody knows what's best for April these days but me." Then she turned and stalked out the door.

Daddy stood there blinking after her like he always did, rubbing at the stubble on his chin.

"I'm sorry," Miss Vest said softly. "I just —"

"No, ma'am," Daddy said with an embarrassed look. "You go ahead and order them shoes for April if you have a mind. Seeing as all the others are getting 'em."

Miss Vest nodded, and Daddy left without another word. Once he had gone, Aunt Birdy sat rocking and shaking her head. For a minute I thought she might make excuses for Mama, maybe even tell Miss Vest all about Riley dying. Part of me wanted her to — just to get it out in the open. I could almost hear in my head how Aunt Birdy would tell it. "It was just after Christmas a little more than a year ago," she would say. "Alma near about died herself from the grief of it. She laid in bed nine days. Wouldn't eat or drink for nine days straight."

Then maybe I would fill in the rest. "On the tenth day she finally got out of bed and dressed herself," I would say, "and Daddy and me just cried, 'cause it seemed like the worst was over." But the worst wasn't over.

Aunt Birdy sat there with her mouth clamped tight. I should have known she wouldn't say a word about Riley to Miss Vest. If she did, Miss Vest would surely ask how he died and my grandmother would have to explain, with me standing two feet away — about how the accident happened when I was home alone taking care of my little brother. About how awful it was . . . how bad his burns were.

Miss Vest stepped toward me. "Do you know what size shoe you wear, April?" she asked quietly.

"No, ma'am," I told her.

She fetched her satchel again and dug around until she found some clean white paper and a thick pencil. Then she had me take my boots off and step right on the paper so she could draw an outline of my feet. My socks probably smelled like our shed and there were pieces of hay prickling out of the yarn, but Miss Vest didn't seem to care. She bent down close to my feet, and I could feel her hands, warm and gentle, through the damp wool.

"There," Miss Vest said when she was done. "The next best thing to going to Chicago and having Mr. Sears measure your foot himself."

"I declare," Aunt Birdy said, her face brightening up again. Then she remembered the catalog in her lap and went back to admiring the pages, holding each one like it was a butterfly wing between her fingers. I went around behind her chair in my stocking feet to watch the pictures flash by — rows of ladies' bonnets and gloves, diamond bracelets and necklaces, baby buggies, furniture, and farm tools.

Toward the back of the book, Aunt Birdy stopped. "Don't tell me you can order a whole house right out of this catalog!" she cried, and leaned down closer to squint at the pictures.

Miss Vest came over to join us. "You sure can," she said. "They send you all the materials to build it. The lumber, the nails, gutters, shingles, paint, varnish — everything. So which one would you like? How about that one there — the Conway Bungalow? It's got five rooms and a bath. And look, you'll have a breakfast alcove and a coal chute and an ironing board that folds out of a cabinet in the wall."

"How much?" Aunt Birdy asked.

"Only one thousand six hundred and four dollars, or you can make low monthly payments of just thirty dollars. What do you think?"

"Heh!" Aunt Birdy crowed, kicking her little feet off the floor. "It sure is pretty but I think I better stick with what I got."

As she flipped to the next page, a thought came to me, and before I even knew I was talking out loud, I said, "I wonder how long it would take me."

Miss Vest turned to look at me. "Take you for what, April?"

I shook my head and tried to laugh a little. "Oh, nothing . . . I was just wondering how long it would take me to, well, to learn to write out an order."

Miss Vest's eyes lit up. "I could teach you in no time, April. But why? Is there something special you'd like to buy?"

"No, ma'am," I said, feeling shy. "I don't have money to buy anything, but still . . . might be fun just to make an order . . . just to think about."

"You mean a wish list," Miss Vest said.

86

I nodded. "That's right. A wish list." The words felt nice on my tongue — hushed, like a secret.

Miss Vest clapped her hands together. "That's a wonderful idea! We could —"

But before she could say anything else, somebody banged on the door.

"Now who's that?" Aunt Birdy asked, pushing herself to her feet and scurrying over to open it. I half expected to see Mama standing in the doorway waiting to fetch me back home, but it was a marine — the one called Sergeant Jordan.

"Sergeant!" Miss Vest cried. "What are you doing here?"

"I've been looking for you all afternoon, ma'am," he told her, taking off his hat. "I've got a message for you from Camp Rapidan. The Hoovers are here for the weekend and would like you to join them tonight for dinner."

Miss Vest's face turned pale. *"Dinner? Tonight?"*

"Yes, ma'am. I tried to let you know earlier, but I couldn't find you. Good thing I ran into Mr. Jessup on the road. He told me you might be down this way."

Miss Vest's hands fluttered up to smooth her hair. "I've been out calling on my students. I didn't even know the Hoovers were coming this weekend."

Sergeant Jordan sighed. "Neither did we, until yesterday. You should see what it's like down at the base. We've all been reassigned to new posts, and everybody's tearing around like crazy trying to —" He blushed and pulled himself up straight again. "Anyway, ma'am, we should probably get going. I'm supposed to have you over at Camp Rapidan by five o'clock."

Miss Vest looked at her wristwatch and let out a gasp. "But — but it's quarter to five now!" She stared down at her skirt and sweater. "Can I at least wash up and change my clothes?"

"Yes, ma'am," Sergeant Jordan told her. "I've got the truck waiting up by the school-house."

Aunt Birdy and I traded looks. *Miss Vest was going to Camp Rapidan.* For months everybody had been gossiping about what was behind those big metal gates down the mountain. Folks said that Mrs. Hoover rode around on her big bay horse wearing a suit of white riding clothes and the president spent all day fishing the trout streams, not even stopping to loosen up his high starched collar and tie. I imagined their summer house probably looked like the biggest one in the Sears, Roebuck catalog, the two-story one with the brick chimneys and the shutters and the porch with the pillars out front.

And now Miss Vest was heading off to see Camp Rapidan for herself. I watched as she flitted around, gathering up her catalog and the outline of my foot and shoving them in her satchel.

"It was so good to meet you, Aunt Birdy," she said, all out of breath. "And April, I'll see you at school on Monday. . . . I'm sorry I have to run off like this. What in the world am I going to wear?" She laughed a high, nervous laugh and touched the tips of her fingers to the bright red spots on her cheeks.

Aunt Birdy and I walked out to the front porch to see her off. Mama and Daddy were still working, stacking wood against the shed over in the side yard. "Goodbye!" Miss Vest called to them. "Hope to see you again soon!"

Daddy waved, but Mama never even looked up from the load of kindling in her arms. I was glad Miss Vest was too riled to notice. As she hurried up the slope behind Sergeant Jordan, she turned around and gave me one last smile. It was all I could do to hold myself back from running up the mountain after her.

Eight

■■■■■■■■■■■■■■■■■■■■■■■■■■■■■

The Hoovers must have invited Miss Vest over so they could ask her to work even harder. Because pretty soon after her dinner at Camp Rapidan, she told the class she planned to start holding Sunday prayer meetings at the schoolhouse. Most of the kids broke out clapping. We had never had a real church on our mountain before. The nearest one was over in Dark Hollow, near eight miles away, with no heat and a leaky roof to boot. So most folks chose to squeeze into the Jessup cabin on Sundays, where Mr. Jessup preached his long, rambling sermons standing on an old kindling box at one end of his front room. Now that their daddy would be helping Miss Vest with worship services at the schoolhouse, Dewey and Ida looked around the classroom grinning and nodding as if the whole thing had been their idea.

I was about the only one who didn't cheer over Miss Vest's announcement. I felt sorry for Miss Vest, having to teach us our letters and numbers and now the Bible, too. I couldn't help worrying over how hard she seemed to be working. After school let out every day, she sat right down at her desk and bent over her lesson book with her face feverish and her ink pen flying. One night I had supper at Aunt Birdy's and took the long way home, just to check, and sure enough, there she was, lit up in the schoolroom window, still sitting at her desk and rubbing her tired eyes.

I didn't even bother to ask Mama if we could go to the Sunday prayer meetings. We hadn't been to church since Riley died. Used to be, we'd all ride in the wagon to go to meetings in Dark Hollow. Once in a while, if the weather was too bad to make it that far, we'd crowd into the Jessup cabin with all the other neighbors. I knew Mama despised those mornings as much as I did. Most of the time, we got stuck sitting back in the sweltering kitchen next to the cookstove, listening to Mr. Jessup rant and rave for an hour or more. We always came home smelling like cabbage or collards or whatever had been bubbling on the burner next to us.

Mr. Jessup wasn't an official preacher anyway. During the week he worked at the sawmill over at Thornton Gap, heaving logs onto the conveyor belt. But on Sundays, he put on his black suit and combed his thick hair back with pomade and turned into someone else. Aunt Birdy said he had learned to preach from traveling men who wandered around the Blue Ridge holding tent meetings and revivals. She said his sermons were hand-me-downs, but even so, Mama and Daddy thought it was important for us to learn the Gospel, so Riley and I went along without complaining.

Then the accident happened and Mama never said another word about going to church. Whenever Aunt Birdy invited us to join her, Mama just shook her head and found a way to change the subject. Daddy didn't try to persuade her otherwise.

So you could have pushed me over with a broom straw one rainy Sunday morning when Mama said after breakfast, "You better get dressed, April. We're going down to the meeting at the schoolhouse."

"Is Daddy coming, too?" I asked. I figured going to church must have been his idea. He had been away all week, helping to fence pastures for a cattle farmer down the mountain. Maybe since it was Sunday, he'd be joining us at the schoolhouse.

But Mama shook her head. "No. It's just us going. Daddy won't be back till tomorrow."

I decided not to ask why we were going. I ran to put on my best dress before Mama could change her mind. My insides were so full of butterflies, I could barely hook up the buttons. *Mama was coming to school.* Finally, she'd get to see how fine everything was — the shelf full of *National Geographic* and *Child Life* magazines, and the world globe that could spin around, and the jars full of rulers and scissors and paintbrushes. Miss Vest had told us that after each Sunday meeting she was planning to serve coffee and hot cocoa. Maybe she'd pick me to add the marshmallows to the cocoa again, and I could serve a cup to Mama.

We didn't bother hitching up Old Dean for the trip over to the schoolhouse. The rain was pounding on the roof like hooves, splattering down to make muddy rivers in the yard. Mama found an old green slicker and I held a shawl over my head, and we set off with a gust of wind blowing at our backs. By the time we made it to the schoolhouse, the classroom was packed full with folks, all dripping wet from the trip over. Miss Vest was scurrying around, mopping at the floor with a rag and setting up folding chairs in between the desks.

She trotted over when she saw us coming, and the next minute Aunt Birdy was at my side, giving my hand a squeeze. "See there, Miss Vest," she said, grinning, "I told you not to give up on 'em. I told you Alma was coming."

Mama and Miss Vest nodded to each other, and then Aunt Birdy scooted us over to three folding chairs in the second row, behind the Jessups. I knew Mama would have rather found a place in the back, but she followed Aunt Birdy without a fuss, trying to ignore all the ladies who stared as she walked by. Most folks hadn't seen her out in company for a year or more, and I wasn't surprised at the way they put their heads together and started clucking like hens.

Mrs. Jessup, who was bouncing Dewey's fat baby brother, Little Elton, on her lap and sizing up everybody who came down the aisle, hoisted herself around and said hello to Mama. "Good to see you out again, Alma," she said in a loud, sugary voice. "Look, Ida . . . Dewey . . . there's April. I hear Wes is working down in Criglersville now. It's been so long since we seen you all. We been looking for you over at our place on Sundays."

Mama nodded, but I knew she was thinking the same thing I was. She'd sooner walk through fire than go to the Jessups' house again, with our Victrola sitting right out in their front room.

Aunt Birdy leaned across me and tapped Mama's arm before Mrs. Jessup could say anything else. "Look over yonder, Alma," she said. "That's where Apry sits ever' day. In that desk where Alvin Hurt is setting. Miss Vest showed me at last Sunday's meeting. And look up there. There's her painting up on the wall, the one of the chestnut trees down the mountain. See, it's got a gold star on the top."

Mrs. Jessup huffed herself back around again, and Mama seemed to relax. She flicked her eyes up to my painting on the bulletin board and tried to manage a smile. "Looks real nice, April," she said, and I smiled back, feeling something flutter in my chest.

I was getting ready to point out some other things around the room when Miss Vest came up to the front and welcomed everybody, sweeping her hands this way and that. She was thrilled to see more new faces each week, she said, glancing at Mama and me. Then she announced that she had decided to start each Sunday with a Bible reading, since that seemed to be everybody's favorite part of the service.

"For today," she said, carefully opening

the Bible, "I've decided to read the passages from Genesis about Noah and his ark. . . . When I selected these, I honestly had no idea we'd be living through our own flood this morning. You all might need an ark to get back home today." Everybody laughed and turned to look at the rain streaking across the windows.

Of course I had heard about old Noah before, but I never knew the whole story until Miss Vest began to read. Nobody had ever told me that Noah was six hundred years old when he made his big floating barn out of gopher wood. And I had never really thought about what it would be like for all those animals to squeeze together, two by two in the ark, with the windows of heaven stuck open and rain pouring down for forty days and forty nights.

I could have sat listening to Miss Vest for at least that long. Her voice was steady and soothing, like the sound of the rainfall outside, and next to me Aunt Birdy closed her eyes and rocked back and forth as she listened. It was like we were all under a spell of some kind in that warm, steamy room, with the smell of Silas Hudgins's pipe tobacco hanging in the air.

I was sorry when Miss Vest closed her Bible. But then she started talking to us about what happened after the flood, how God had used the rains to make the world clean and new again. Her words kept humming through my head, even when folks started standing up, one at a time, saying prayers for their kin. Effie Kerns asked the Lord to heal her sister's youngest, who had taken sick with scarlet fever. Somebody else had a father with palsy. And after each person finished speaking, we all said "Amen," and it felt powerful, as if that one little word could truly help make the sick folks well.

And then the strangest thing happened. All of a sudden, it was me who was standing up, rising to my feet in front of that whole room full of people. All of a sudden, it was me saying right out loud, "God, please watch over my little brother, Riley, up in heaven and please help Mama and Daddy and me —"

But I never got to finish. Right then, I felt a sharp poke, like a broom handle, in my side. And I turned just in time to see Mama pulling her hand away. Her face was hard and blank as stone. But she had done it. She had jabbed me with all her might, cutting my words off at the quick. I stood there, wobbling, trying to decide what to do next, but there was no way I could finish after that. I sat down hard and stared at my lap, feeling my cheeks burning red.

"Amen, April," I heard Miss Vest say, and a few others joined in, their voices all soft and nervous. They must have seen what Mama had done.

I couldn't look at her. All I could do was squeeze my fists tighter and tighter, hearing those same ugly words I had been saying to myself for more than a year, *"She hates me. . . . She loved Riley best and now she's stuck with me. . . . She hates me."*

And there was no denying it — she would hate me more if she knew what *really* had happened that night.

After the accident, when all the questions came, when everybody started asking, "What happened, April? Where were you? What happened?" *I had lied.* Before I even knew what was coming out of my mouth, I found myself lying. I told Mama and Daddy the fire had been getting low and we were awful cold and that I had gone out back to fetch another log from the woodpile. Riley must have been trying to stoke the fire himself, I said, and by the time I came back inside and threw the quilt over his little body, it was too late.

But that wasn't the way it had really happened.

Aunt Birdy's hand crept over and caught hold of mine. That's when my eyes started filling up with tears. I was too ashamed to wipe them away, so they rolled down my face and dropped onto the back of Aunt Birdy's wrinkly hand.

I finally lifted my head when Miss Vest called Preacher Jessup up to say his piece. But looking at the Jessups, beaming at their daddy from the front row, only made me feel worse. Mrs. Jessup kept leaning over to kiss Little Elton's fat cheek, and Dewey was wearing his new brown wool suit — the one he had bought down at Taggart's with all the money the reporters had given him.

To make things worse, Mr. Jessup had started to rock back and forth on his heels, like he always did when he was getting worked up for one of his sermons. I knew he would probably preach for an hour or more, his words pouring out smooth as melted butter. He'd wave his hands through the air and bang the Bible against his chest, going on and on about scary-sounding things like Judgment Day and souls lost to the ways of sloth.

I felt like a bird I had seen once trapped in the rafters of our shed, beating its head and wings against the boards. I leaned over to tell Aunt Birdy that I was headed to the bathroom. But just as I tapped her arm, I heard the door in the back of the classroom open.

Mr. Jessup stopped rocking. His eyes got wide, and soon everybody was turning around to see what he was staring at.

Standing in the doorway was an older man dressed in city clothes — in a dark gray hat and a three-piece gray suit and starched collar. I had seen him before, but I couldn't remember where until I heard somebody in the room let out a gasp. Then Aunt Birdy said, "Well, look a'there," and all of a sudden, I knew.

Still, just to be sure, I turned around and double-checked the big framed picture hanging over the chalkboard . . . the stiff collar, the serious face, the steady gray eyes.

It was him all right — President Herbert Hoover. And following along behind was his wife, Lou Henry Hoover, and behind her were two marine guards. The marines stepped into the doorway and stood with their hands behind their backs, gazing out over the schoolroom.

For a minute, everybody froze. Then, all at once, the room was full of chattering and whispering, and Miss Vest was springing up from her chair. "Hello!" she cried, hurrying down the aisle. "I got the message that you might come, but I never thought you'd be able to make it up here in this weather. Welcome, Mr. President! Good morning, Mrs. Hoover!"

"Good morning to *you,*" the president said, looking around, with the corners of his mouth twitching into a smile. We must have been a sight, all gawping at him with our jaws hanging open. He took off his hat, shaking drops of rain from the brim. Then he searched around for a place to set his umbrella.

Miss Vest rushed up to take it, but Mrs. Hoover shooed her away. "Please, Miss Vest," she said. "Don't let us interrupt any longer. We're so sorry to be late. The muddy roads took a bit longer to navigate than we thought."

Miss Vest shook her head. "It's quite all right! You've arrived at a perfect time. Mr. Jessup was just getting ready to begin his sermon. Please . . . please sit down." She flitted back to the front of the room to a pair of folding chairs propped against the wall next to her own. "Here. Here are some seats I saved for you," she said.

Mr. Jessup hurried over to help set the chairs into place along the wall, and I heard him say in a hoarse voice, "I can leave my sermon till next week, Miss Vest. It might be best, you know, seeing as we didn't expect the Hoovers here and all."

"No, Mr. Jessup," she whispered back. "You just go right ahead like we planned. The Hoovers didn't want us to make any fuss or change our routine."

He frowned and looked over at his wife, but Mrs. Jessup was busy handing Little Elton off to Ida and smoothing her dress over her knees.

As the Hoovers walked down the aisle to their seats, a few men reached out to shake the president's hand. Mrs. Hoover greeted everybody, acting like she didn't even notice all the women stretching their necks to get an eyeful of her flower-print dress and her smart hat. The name, first lady, suited her, the way she glided along, smiling and murmuring, "How do you do? . . . Pleased to see you. . . . How do you do?"

I couldn't help sneaking a glance over at Mama to see what she was thinking. Our eyes met — just for a second. Then Mama looked away and so did I, and we sat there quiet, waiting for everyone to get settled while Aunt Birdy perched on the edge of her seat like a little girl.

Once the Hoovers had taken their chairs against the side wall, Miss Vest came back to stand at the front of the room. "I'm sure everyone here," she said, turning to smile at the Hoovers, "would like to convey how thrilled and happy we are to have you with us this morning. Of course, if it weren't for your generosity, this fine schoolhouse and these children and their families wouldn't be here today."

Everybody broke out clapping, and the Hoovers bobbed their heads and smiled till the room turned quiet again. Then Miss Vest said, "So now without further delay, I'll let Mr. Elton Jessup get on with his sermon."

Mr. Jessup stepped to the front of the room. I waited for him to take a deep breath like usual and start in with "Brothers and sisters . . ." But as soon as he lifted his head, we could all tell something was wrong. His face had turned gray, like the color of dirty dishwater, and his forehead was shiny with sweat. And he didn't say a word. Just stood there, blinking and swallowing with his Adam's apple working up and down in his throat. I could see Dewey squirming in his seat, wondering what was the matter.

"*Elton?*" Mrs. Jessup called faintly.

Her husband glanced down at her and gave a puny little laugh. "Nobody told me the president was coming today," he said. His voice sounded lost, nothing like the swelled-up voice we were all used to.

Then Mr. Jessup looked over at Miss Vest, who had taken her place next to the Hoovers. "Why didn't you tell me?" he asked. "If I'da known they were coming, I would have planned something special."

Miss Vest stared back, helpless. She opened her mouth to answer, then shut it when Mr. Jessup slowly turned to the Hoovers.

"I would have planned something special," he said again. " 'Course, I had plenty to say today about the Scripture we heard, and well, about the paths to salvation. . . . But everything just ran right out my head when you walked in here."

A chunk of Preacher Jessup's slick hair had fallen down on his forehead. He didn't even try to push it away. "I reckon you've heard some fine speeches in your life, sir," he said to the president.

From where I sat, I could see President Hoover lean forward in his chair as if he and Mr. Jessup were the only two people in the room. "Yes, and I've heard some mighty dreadful ones, too, Mr. Jessup," he told him. "I come from a Quaker background, so my favorite sermons are the simplest — straight from the heart."

Mr. Jessup nodded for a long time,

looking down at his feet. "That's real good advice, sir," he finally answered. "I won't be forgetting it any time soon. But for now, I reckon I just . . . just better say thank you and head on out of here before I make a bigger jackass of myself." And before we knew what was happening, he was walking softly down the aisle, excusing himself as he pushed past the marines and slid out the door.

The door swung shut behind him, and there was a second of awful quiet until Mrs. Jessup started getting to her feet, too. We could all hear her nagging at Dewey and Ida. "Come on now," she hissed. "We got to go after your pa. . . . *Come on.*" She yanked Little Elton out of Ida's arms, and headed after Mr. Jessup, with her eyes blazing and her kids trailing after her.

Dewey was the last one to follow. As he walked by, he kept his head down and his hands shoved in his pockets. He looked shamed to the bone. I know I should have felt bad for him, but I didn't. Not one little bit. I felt glad — glad that Dewey Jessup was finally seeing what it felt like to have folks staring and feeling sorry for him.

Miss Vest looked weary, as if all her weeks of trying so hard were finally catching up to her. Somehow she managed to announce that it was time for the closing hymn, "Bringing In the Sheaves." Without a fiddle or even a mouth organ to keep us in tune, our singing sounded pitiful. Miss Vest and Aunt Birdy and Mrs. Hoover were about the only ones who knew all the words, and the rest of us limped along in scratchy voices.

After we were done, everybody rushed up to the front of the room to shake hands with the Hoovers, like nothing with Mr. Jessup had ever happened. Aunt Birdy pulled me into line, saying, "Come on, Apry. Don't you want to meet the president?"

I nodded, trying not to watch Mama as she slipped away through the crowd and out the door.

Nine

■■■■■■■■■■■■■■■■■■■■■■■■■■■

I was spending recess under my chestnut tree the next week when Poke McClure turned up out of nowhere. One minute I was sitting by myself trying to make out words in a little book Miss Vest had loaned me. The next minute, I turned around to find Poke slouched against the tree behind me.

"You learned to read yet?" he asked, eyeing the book spread across my lap. It was filled with pictures of a brother and sister smiling and feeding their new kitten and putting her to sleep in a straw basket.

I squinted up at Poke through the bright afternoon sun. He looked even meaner than I remembered, with his dirty hands hitched over the straps of his overalls and a shadow of black fuzz growing along his sharp jaw. I didn't know whether to answer him or not.

"Well?" he asked again.

"Almost," I lied. I bent over my book and pretended to start reading again.

Poke grunted and glared out at the schoolyard, where Ida and her friends were busy skipping rope and chanting the sing-song rhymes that Miss Vest had been teaching them: "Mabel, Mabel . . . set the table . . . just as fast as . . . you are able."

I looked around for Miss Vest, then remembered she was still inside, clearing a space in the classroom for the new piano. The piano had arrived just that morning, right in the middle of our arithmetic lesson. It had been sent as a present for the school from a musical instrument company. All the kids were so excited that Miss Vest had to ask the delivery men to roll the piano into her parlor for the time being — at least until we finished our lessons for the day.

"Hey! Look who's here!" I heard somebody yell.

A few boys had spotted Poke leaning against the tree. They let the ball they were playing with drop to the ground. I wasn't surprised when Dewey came strolling over. He was still wearing his wool suit, even though it needed a cleaning and the day was plenty warm enough for short sleeves.

"Hey there, Poke," he said. "You get tired of clearing stumps and decide to come back to school?"

Poke settled back into the crook of the tree, crossing his arms and sizing up Dewey's knickers. "Naw," he said, drawing out his words long and slow. "You won't be seeing me at school again. . . . But I might start coming to those Sunday meetings. From what I hear down at Taggart's, the sermons are getting a lot shorter these days."

A sickly look flicked over Dewey's face, and then he muttered, "Last Sunday weren't Pa's fault. Miss Vest should have told him the Hoovers were coming."

Poke let out a mean little laugh. "Huh! The way I figure it, Miss Vest and old President Hoover did folks round here a favor with that little surprise visit."

Poke didn't see Dewey's hands curling into fists. He was too busy smirking and showing off for all the kids who had started to crowd around the chestnut. "Maybe now," he said in a louder voice, "Preacher Jessup might stick to logging, where he belongs."

He had barely gotten the words out before Dewey was on top of him like a wildcat. They fell to the ground, and all I could see was a tangle of elbows and knees and punches and kicks. Then I heard Ida screaming, "Stop it, Poke! Stop it! Somebody run get Miss Vest. Poke McClure's gonna kill my brother!"

I crawled out of the way on all fours,

leaving my book behind me in the dust, but with all the kids pushing closer to see, I could barely get clear of the fighting. Finally, I managed to scrabble to my feet just in time to see Dewey, with his lip split and his nose bloody and his eyes full of the devil, lunging at Poke again. All of a sudden, both boys were barreling toward me, and before I could get free they sent me slamming backward into the gnarled roots of the tree.

I managed to throw my hands back to catch myself, but when I landed, I heard a funny pop and felt a pain like a pitchfork driving into my arm. I was afraid to look down, afraid of seeing a bone splintering up through my skin. My ears filled with a roaring, so loud that I couldn't hear the kids around me anymore. I rolled over on my side, hugging my hurt arm. The next thing I knew, Luella was peering down at me, and then Alvin and Dewey with his fat lip. Then I saw their feet shuffling backward, trying to make room. Soon Miss Vest was kneeling in the dirt beside me, out of breath, asking me the same questions over and over.

After a few moments, her words started to make sense. "Answer me, April," she said, sounding sterner than I'd ever heard her. "Tell me where it hurts."

"My arm," I whispered. "I think it's broke." It was hard to talk with my tongue and lips caked with dust. All I wanted was a drink of cold water, and then maybe I'd feel better. I tried to sit up, but the pain came washing over me again, making me sick to my stomach. I dropped back in the nest of roots.

"That's all right," Miss Vest said. "Just lie still for now." She got to her feet and I heard her say, "Ida, you stay here while I run inside and telephone Sergeant Jordan to bring the truck up from the marine camp. We need to get April down to a doctor in the valley. . . . The rest of you children, try and give her some room."

Once Miss Vest had hurried off and most of the other kids had started to drift away, Ida and Luella stood with their arms crossed, staring down at me.

"So where'd that nasty Poke run off to?" Ida asked Luella.

"He hightailed it for the woods soon as he saw Miss Vest coming."

"I think I must have knocked one of his front teeth out," Dewey said. He was leaning against the tree, studying a cut on his knuckles.

Ida looked disgusted. "You're a sight, Dewey," she said, glaring at the streaks of dirt and sweat on her brother's face and the ripped pocket of his jacket. "Wait till Mama sees that suit and finds out you been fighting with Poke McClure. And wait till she sees the doctor's bill she's gonna owe for taking care of *her*."

Ida's voice turned sour when she said *her*, like she had just swallowed bad milk. She acted like I wasn't even there, lying right at her feet listening. I gritted my dusty teeth together as hard as I could and pushed myself up to my knees with my good arm.

"Hush up, Ida," Dewey snapped. "Can't you see her arm's broke?" He came over to squat beside me, so close that I could see a smear of blood drying under his nose. "Shouldn't you stay put till Miss Vest gets back, April?"

Hearing Dewey say my real name made me even madder. He hadn't called me anything but ghost girl for more than a year, and now here he was trying to cozy up to me just so he wouldn't get in trouble. And what would Mama say? At least it wasn't my right arm, the one I mostly used for chores and writing. I squeezed my eyes shut and stood up all the way, hugging my hurt arm and trying to fight back the ripples of dizziness in my head.

Just then Miss Vest came running back. "April, wait," she said. "Let me help you before you make things worse. . . . I called Dr. Hunt, but he's away at a conference in Charlottesville all week, so the medical aide from the marine camp is coming. At least he can take a look and tell us whether you need a cast or not."

She started steering me back to the schoolhouse. Then she stopped and gave Dewey a hard look over her shoulder. "Come on, Dewey. After I get April and everyone else settled inside, you and I need to have a talk."

I had never been in Miss Vest's parlor before, but for once I didn't care about examining every inch of another room at the schoolhouse. My arm felt so strange and achy, I leaned my head against the back of the davenport and kept my eyes closed until the man from the marine camp arrived. He said he was "Lou Witcofski, hospital corpsman." But even though he carried a black bag, he didn't look like a doctor or even a doctor's helper. More than anything, he reminded me of an overgrown puppy with his friendly face and his long, loose legs and arms.

He was tall enough to make everything in Miss Vest's parlor seem small — the wide, stuffed davenport and the high walnut rockers, even the new piano that sat out in the middle of the room.

"Sorry about the furniture arrangement," Miss Vest said as Corpsman Witcofski squeezed his lanky body around the piano to reach me. "I'm still trying to find a place for this in the classroom."

"I think it's fine right here," he said and pulled up the piano bench in front of the davenport where I was sitting. "Just what I need. An examining chair."

Miss Vest smiled. "Will you two be all right for a few minutes while I go check on things in the classroom?"

I nodded even though I wasn't so sure, but then the man told me to call him Wit, since Witcofski was too hard to say, and he leaned forward and whispered, "If you promise not to be nervous, I'll play you a song on that new piano when I'm done."

I nodded again.

Wit turned serious as soon as he started looking over my arm. He asked me to try and straighten it, but I couldn't even move a couple inches without yelping.

"Easy now," he said and took my arm in both of his big square hands. Then he ran his fingers along my forearm like he was stroking a cat's back. "It's broken, all right," he told me. "Right about there." He

114

pointed to a spot halfway between my wrist and my elbow.

"We'll put a splint on it for now, until we can get you down to see the doctor. He'll want to take an X-ray and put a proper cast on."

Then Wit reached into his black bag and brought out rolls of bandages and white tape and some wooden splints, and went to work. He kept asking me questions while he fiddled with my arm, trying to keep my mind off the pain, I suppose.

"What's your favorite color?" he asked.

"Blue," I told him.

"Any blue? What kind of blue?"

"The robin's egg kind."

"Any brothers and sisters?"

I shook my head.

"What's your favorite food?"

"Fried apple pie."

"Mmm. That sounds good."

And before long he had my arm wrapped up tight like a package and hanging in a muslin sling tied around my neck.

When he was done, he rubbed his hands together and swung his long legs to the other side of the piano bench. "What'll it be, miss?" he said over his shoulder. "You held up your end of the bargain. Now it's my turn."

"You pick," I said, feeling shy.

He swept his thumbnail along the piano keys, making a long rippling sound that floated higher and higher. "How about this?" Then all at once his fingers were dancing and bouncing and hopping, and one hand was crossing over the other. Even though my arm was aching, I couldn't help pushing myself up from the davenport and going over to stand beside him to watch. I never thought I'd hear music finer than what I had heard on our Victrola, but I was wrong.

Then he was done. Since I couldn't clap, I just stood there grinning. Wit laughed and started packing his bandages and tape into his black bag. He had just snapped the clasp shut when Miss Vest rushed in.

"I'm sorry that took so long," she said all in a fluster. "Did I hear the piano —"

Then her eyes landed on my sling and her face filled with worry. "It's broken?"

Wit nodded. "I think so. I'm hoping that the splint and sling will hold the bone in the right place until you can get her down to see a doctor." He reached in his pocket and pulled out a little jar of pills. "You can give her two of these every four hours for the pain."

"Good," Miss Vest said. "And April, I

think you should stay with me tonight. I'll send Dewey down to tell your mother."

I stared at Miss Vest, wondering whether I had heard right. "You want me to sleep *here* tonight? At the *schoolhouse?*"

"Yes," she said. "There's a spare bedroom upstairs, and I'm sure your mother won't want you walking all the way home when you just broke your arm."

"Well, I guess I'd better be getting back to camp," Wit said. He patted the top of the piano on his way out. "Fine instrument you got here."

Miss Vest sighed. "I know. Too bad the teacher doesn't play a single note."

"Oh, really?" Wit raised one eyebrow.

"From what I heard earlier, you're very good."

"Oh, I play a little," he said. Then he looked down at me and winked. "Let me know if you have any more questions about April's arm . . . or about your piano."

When Wit had gone, Miss Vest reached out and touched my sling, her fingers light as rain. "I'm so sorry, April," she said. "I'd give anything for this not to have happened."

I nodded, but down deep, I couldn't help being glad. A broken arm was a small price to pay for a night with Miss Vest at the schoolhouse.

Ten

Miss Vest's tub was wide and deep, more like a swimming hole than a place just meant for washing. It had smooth, slippery sides and fancy curved legs and a little step stool ready to help you climb inside. I couldn't wait to lean back against that white porcelain. The only problem was I had to get undressed first — in front of Miss Vest. With my arm in the sling and all the gadgets, like one faucet for hot water and another for cold and the little rubber stopper on a chain, there was no chance I could figure everything out by myself.

But somehow Miss Vest made it easy. She kept chatting away as the water climbed higher and higher in the tub and the room fogged up, and we worked off my sling, then my sweater and my shirt and my skirt with the ripped pocket, and finally my underclothes. Then Miss Vest wrapped a towel around my bandaged splint to keep it dry and poured a dollop of lavender oil in the running water, all the while telling me about how she and her little sister used to take

118

baths in a big wooden washtub outdoors, behind her farmhouse in the summer. She said they pretended they were fairy princesses, and picked daisies and bee balm and pink roses from their mother's garden to float on top of the bath water.

When I was ready, Miss Vest helped me into the tub, making sure that I rested my wrapped-up arm on the dry porcelain. It felt so good sinking down into all that steamy heat that I almost forgot about being naked in front of my teacher. She bustled back and forth, setting out soap and another towel and one of her very own nightgowns for me to borrow. Then she turned off the faucets and said she'd leave me to soak for a while. "Call me when you're ready to come out," she told me.

It felt strange just lying still in the water, watching my fingers and toes wrinkle up like tree bark. At home, Riley and I never wanted to set in the old metal washtub for long. The half-warm water Mama poured in made us shiver, and chips of rust were always rubbing off the bottom of the tub and floating to the top.

I wondered whether Mama was worried about me at all. I hoped she was, just a little, I took a deep breath of the sweet, thick lavender steam rising off the water and smiled to myself. I would smell like Miss Vest tonight, and after today, Mama couldn't help but be grateful to her for taking such good care of me.

I glanced over at the nightgown she had left folded on the step stool. It was white flannel with silk blue ribbon laces at the neck. I couldn't wait to put it on. I didn't want to bother Miss Vest, so I climbed out of the tub by myself as careful as I could. It took me such a long time to dry off and work the nightgown over my head and bandaged arm that I had to stop to rest for a minute afterward. But even though the sleeves of the nightgown were too long and the bottom dragged the floor, the flannel felt warm and snug as a cocoon.

I hurried over to the mirror and tried to wipe away the steam with the towel, hoping to get a better look at myself. But the mirror kept fogging over so I finally gave up and started studying Miss Vest's lipsticks and tiny pots of rouge and powder lined up on the shelf above the sink. I picked out a little gold case, and being sure to hold my broken arm steady, I opened the lid with my good hand. Inside there was a tiny flat brush and tin filled with something black and sooty.

I dipped the brush into the tin and was standing there puzzling over what it could be used for when Miss Vest walked in. She stopped in the doorway looking surprised.

"I'm sorry!" I said, rushing to fit the brush back into the case. I was so clumsy that I jabbed it against my fingers instead, smearing them with the black soot. "I didn't mean to get into your things," I said. "I was just — I was —"

Miss Vest only smiled. She walked over and took the gold case from me. Then she said, "Hold still," and she started painting my eyelashes with the little brush, leaning close and biting the side of her lip as she worked. When she was done, she turned me around to face the mirror. I could see myself now that the door was open and the glass had cleared.

"Lordy," was all I could say. I looked close to pretty with my cheeks still pink from the bath and my white eyelashes turned as thick and black as Ida's. Miss Vest found a comb and started fluffing up the wispy pieces of hair around my face, and for a while I couldn't take my eyes off the person in the mirror.

All of a sudden, we heard Aunt Birdy calling, and Miss Vest ran to fetch her. "Dewey just came by to tell me," I heard Aunt Birdy saying in a breathless voice from the parlor. "How is she?"

"Come on back and see for yourself," Miss Vest told her.

Aunt Birdy's eyes got wide when she came in the bathroom and laid eyes on me. "Why, Apry Sloane," she cried, "you look just like the doll baby in Taggart's window."

She fussed and fiddled over my eyelashes and the laces of my nightgown and my sling for a while. Then Miss Vest led us up a tiny flight of stairs to a little bedroom she called "the guest quarters."

"Climb in," Miss Vest said, pointing to one of the beds with a dotted yellow spread and a puffy blanket folded at one end. Before long, she and Aunt Birdy had me tucked into the soft sheets and satiny blanket, with my broken arm resting on top of a feather pillow. I was sure I would never fall asleep with the strangeness of it all. But before she said good night, Miss Vest brought me two more pills with a glass of water and she pulled a rocker up close to my bed. Aunt Birdy sat down, and I finally drifted off to the sounds of her creaky rocking and humming beside me.

I woke up to voices — angry and low at the bottom of the stairs. The voices had worked their way into my dream, something about me and Dewey fighting over the picture book I had left under the chestnut tree. It seemed like we had been fighting for hours, circling round and round each other, our words turning meaner and meaner, just on the edge of something terrible.

I pushed myself up in bed, trying to get my bearings. *My arm.* Somehow it had tangled up in the sling and the long sleeve of my nightgown, and now it hurt so bad I wanted to whimper. But then I heard those voices again and footsteps on the stairs and I knew it was Mama.

Before I could get out of bed, she was flying into the room with Miss Vest following along behind her. Miss Vest looked like she had just woke up, with her eyes still puffy from sleep and her wavy hair mashed to one side. She had on a long blue robe tied at the middle.

"Please, Mrs. Sloane, wait," Miss Vest called. "Just let me explain something. . . ."

"No, I heard enough," Mama said, marching over to take my broken arm in her hands. Her fingers felt as cold and hard as barbed wire. Without even glancing at my face, she started peeling away my sling and unwrapping the bandages.

"Her arm's all swolled up," she said, peering down between the splints.

Miss Vest hurried over to see. "I'll get an-

123

other ice pack," she said.

Mama looked shocked. "*Ice pack.* The only thing *ice* is gonna do is drive a chill right down inside that bone."

"But Mrs. Sloane, the corpsman told us —"

Mama whirled around to face Miss Vest. She gritted her teeth like she was chewing dirt. "I . . . don't . . . care . . ." she said, spitting out each word, "what that *corpsman* or whatever he is has to say. He's *wrong* — and this should never have happened in the first place. What kind of school are you running here, where kids are fighting and my daughter gets her arm broke and then doesn't come home all night?"

Miss Vest opened her mouth to answer, but Mama turned away. "Now, come on April," she said. "Get dressed. We're going home."

"But Mama —" I cried.

She shook her head hard, cutting me off. "Where are your clothes?"

"Here," Miss Vest said quietly, lifting the stack of my folded things from the dresser. My heart sank as she turned and went downstairs.

There was nothing I could do to calm Mama down. She wouldn't hear a word — not about Camp Rapidan or the ice packs or

Wit, nothing. While I sat on the bed floppy as a rag doll, she yanked on my stockings and my boots and my sweater, keeping her mouth set in its hard little line. I let my arm hang limp at my side, not even wincing when Mama kept bumping against my splints.

Miss Vest was at the front door of the schoolhouse, waiting to meet us. She held out my sling and the bandages along with the bottle of white pills. "This medicine is for the pain," she said. "April should take two pills every four hours. I'm sure if she keeps to that schedule, she'll feel well enough to come back to school tomorrow."

Mama took the sling and bandages, but she wouldn't touch the pills. "We won't be needing those," she said. "And April won't be coming back to school tomorrow, neither."

Miss Vest forced herself to smile. "Well, the next day then," she said.

Mama let out a heavy sigh, and I knew, with a panic rising in my throat, what was coming. "No, not the next day," she said slowly, like she was talking to a baby. "Ma'am, I thank you for your trouble, but April won't be coming back to your school after today."

Miss Vest blinked. "What do you mean?"

she asked, trying to reach for my mother's sleeve. Her voice was climbing higher. "Mrs. Sloane, we can always decide about school later, but April — she needs medical attention soon. We need to make sure she gets a cast and . . ."

I didn't hear the rest. Mama was herding me through the front door and down the porch steps. It was a fine day, with a gaudy blue sky and a morning sun so bright it seemed to be throbbing, just like the pain in my arm.

Mama kept pushing me along, saying, "Come on now. You'll be better off at home."

I looked over my shoulder at the schoolhouse just once. Miss Vest was standing on the front porch, staring after us, with the tie on her robe flapping in the breeze.

As we passed the chestnut tree, I noticed my little reading book still lying in the dirt. For a second I was tempted to jerk away from Mama, to run and pick it up. At least it would give me something to hold on to. Then I changed my mind. I wouldn't ever want to set eyes on those pages again. All I would see were words I couldn't read and a sister and brother looking so much happier than me.

Eleven

Miss Vest let a week pass before she came knocking. It was awful to sit inside the cabin not making a sound while my teacher pleaded and banged on the rough boards of our door long enough to scrape her knuckles raw.

"Please, Mrs. Sloane," she called out again and again. "Just let me see April for a minute. I won't try to make her come back to school. I just want to see if she's all right. *Please!*"

Still, Mama wouldn't let me open the door. Somehow, with her stare, she forced me to sit frozen like a scared jackrabbit. The second time Miss Vest came, we were in the middle of mucking out the shed when we heard her calling. Mama had been shoveling up manure into a cart while I scattered fresh hay with my good arm.

"Don't you move," Mama warned through her teeth, and I leaned against Old Dean's warm flank, praying for Miss Vest to just give up and go away.

Maybe if Daddy had been around, he

could have stopped Mama from acting so crazy. But he wasn't due back from his latest job for another two weeks. And the truth was, if I had really wanted, I could have run yelling from the shed. *"I'm here!"* I would have screamed. *"My arm's still hurting bad, Miss Vest. What should I do?"*

I can't say for sure why I didn't do it — probably because for the first time in months, Mama was paying attention to me. We didn't talk much, but she was always close. She brewed comfrey leaves and other herbs for poultices to press against my arm. Every morning she checked my sling and my splints, and during the day, when I fumbled through my chores one-handed, I could feel her watching me, worrying.

With Daddy gone, we lit the lantern and sat together at the kitchen table every night, keeping each other company. Mama mended clothes while I tried to cut out scraps of cloth for a crazy quilt that I wanted to make once my arm healed.

One night when Mama was fishing around in the rag bag searching for a piece of cloth to patch Daddy's overalls, I saw her pull out an old shirt of Riley's. I remembered him wearing it buttoned up to the neck on church days. It was soft and faded plaid and looked tiny lying across Mama's lap.

She stared down at it for a minute, her scissors frozen in the air. I held my breath, waiting to see what she would do.

"Don't cut it, Mama," I finally whispered, half expecting her to slice into it anyway just to get rid of it so she'd never have to look at it again.

But when Mama turned toward me, her face looked almost peaceful in the dim light of the oil lamp. "All right," she said, holding the little shirt out. "You take it. Might be nice to work a patch or two into your quilt."

I smiled. It was the first time Mama had ever shared a piece of what she remembered with me. So a week later, when Miss Vest came knocking and pleading again, I decided not to open the door even though I was in the house alone. After that, she didn't come back anymore.

Summer took me by surprise. I had stayed so close to our hollow all spring, I was amazed when Daddy came home saying work was hard to come by with the farmers in the valley so worried about drought.

Then I remembered it hadn't rained since that day in early May when the Hoovers came to the Sunday prayer meeting. But living in our hollow under Doubletop, with the mountain blocking out the sun most of the day, the ground around our cabin still felt damp and spongy under my bare feet. And the spring was running fine, plenty enough to water our vegetable patch up in the clearing.

Still, Daddy stood on the porch, shaking his head and saying it was going to be a long summer. That's when it hit me. "Do you know what the date is?" I asked in a rush.

Daddy gave me a strange look. "June. The twentieth," he said. "Why?"

"Just wondering," I told him, trying to keep my voice calm. But inside, I felt my stomach turn queasy. *June.* I remembered Miss Vest telling the class that school let out in June. We'd all have a break from our lessons, she had said, and she planned to spend her three months of vacation with her family in Kentucky. What if she had left already?

The next day, Mama was so busy lining up chores for Daddy she barely noticed me heading out the door. "I'll be weeding up at the clearing," I called as I grabbed the hoe next to the back step. I started up the path toward the garden, then veered off into the woods, leaving my hoe in the crook of a tree. Then I ran, not even stopping to check the stones in the creek for Aunt Birdy like usual. I wasn't wearing the sling anymore, but my arm still ached sometimes and I had to keep it bent against my side while I ran, like a broken wing.

By the time I started up the last slope toward the schoolyard, sweat was trickling down between my shoulder blades. At the top of the hill, I stopped, hugging my arm and squinting against the baking sun.

I was too late. With the blinds drawn down, the schoolhouse looked naked and lonely. The yard had been swept clean of lunch pails and balls and jump ropes. It was so still, I could hear a squirrel scrabbling through the bare branches of the chestnut. Off in the distance, the mountains stretched out in quiet green waves.

I wandered up to the front steps and stared at the clumps of pink petunias Miss Vest must have planted before she left. They needed watering. I knelt down and yanked at a couple dandelions that had pushed their way up through the drooping flowers. The tops kept snapping off in my hands.

Miss Vest had given up on me, all right. She must have planted her flower bed with Ida or Luella or one of the other girls. Now she was off in Kentucky for the whole summer, maybe for good, and I hadn't even told her goodbye.

★ ★ ★

I found Aunt Birdy back behind her house, hanging out washing. As soon as she saw me, she dropped her clothespins and ran over to give me a squeeze. "I've been waiting for you to come round," she said, pressing her wrinkled cheek against mine.

"I can't stay long," I told her. "Mama thinks I'm out back weeding."

Aunt Birdy shook her head. After I had broken my arm, she had come to visit me a few times. But whenever she told Mama what she thought of me quitting school, Mama had pressed her lips together tight and refused to answer. On her last visit, Aunt Birdy got so disgusted, she left, not even pulling the door closed behind her.

Now she was staring at my arm. "Still hurting you, ain't it?"

I looked down and realized I had been rubbing at the sore spot without even knowing it.

"Not much," I lied and just to show her, I used my bad arm to pull a wet apron from the basket at her feet and pin it on the line with the wooden clothespins.

Aunt Birdy fastened one of her faded cotton dresses next to the apron. "Barely need to hang these up before they're dry," she said. "If it doesn't rain soon, I'm gonna lose my corn. Can't seem to keep anything watered long enough to do any good."

I bent over the basket again, trying to keep my face hidden. "It looks like school's let out," I said.

"That's right. Miss Vest left near a week ago. They took her down to catch the train in Charlottesville."

I couldn't stand it. Aunt Birdy sounded almost cheerful. She chatted on about Miss Vest inviting her over to hear the radio before she left. Then, while we pinned the rest of the clothes up, she started telling me the whole story of the *Amos 'n' Andy* program they had listened to together.

Finally, I couldn't keep quiet anymore. I cut right into the middle of her tale. "Didn't Miss Vest say anything before she left? I mean, anything about *me?*"

Aunt Birdy stopped and gave me a sad little smile. "Why sure she did, honey. I was just getting ready to show you." She took the leftover clothespins from my hands and dropped them into the basket. "Here, come with me," she said and I followed her through her wilty garden back to the house.

Aunt Birdy's place felt like a cave after the glare outside. For a minute I had to stand in the doorway blinking until the corners of the room came clear with their dusty bunches of herbs and ginseng root hanging from the ceiling. Aunt Birdy fished around on a cluttered shelf by the fireplace. When she turned back to me, she was holding out a plain cardboard box.

"She left this for you," she said quietly.

I took the box and stood for a few more seconds, pressing my hand against the smooth lid, trying to make the tingly feeling in my chest last a little longer.

Aunt Birdy squirmed like she had an itch. *"Apry,"* she huffed, "go on and open it."

I laughed, and careful as I could, I pulled off the lid, then pushed aside a rustling layer of tissue paper. Underneath was a pair of beautiful boots, soft leather with low heels and thin laces tied up to the ankle. My breath caught in my throat.

"Lady's slippers!" I said.

"What's that?" Aunt Birdy asked.

"Oh, just something Daddy taught me." I hurried over to the rocker to try on my new shoes. But before I could yank off my sweaty old boots, Aunt Birdy said, "Wait. There's something else." Then she handed me another package wrapped in brown paper and tied with white string. It was heavy.

"There's more?" I said. How could I have thought Miss Vest had forgotten me?

I pulled one end of the string and there on

134

my lap was a thick Sears, Roebuck catalog, along with a pad of clean white paper and a silver ink pen.

I looked up at Aunt Birdy, full of wondering. She shrugged before I could even say anything. "I don't know, Apry," she said. "All she told me was to remind you about your wish list. She said you'd remember."

I sat puzzling for a minute. "I do remember," I said. "I remember telling her it might be fun to write out an order, just for pretend, and she called that a wish list. But I thought we'd be doing it together. She knows I can't read and write good enough to make one on my own."

I flipped through the catalog, feeling the excitement drain out of me again. There was row after row of tiny black print and numbers. I searched for little words I could recognize, but the more pages I turned, the more the letters seemed to swim together in one long black line.

I slammed the catalog shut. "Even if I could read, Mama would never let me keep this catalog. And what about *those*?" I glanced down at the beautiful new boots peeking out of their nest of tissue paper, suddenly realizing how useless they were. "Remember how mad Mama got that day when Miss Vest came here and asked about ordering new shoes? She won't let me step foot inside the house with those fancy boots on."

Aunt Birdy sighed. She reached over and pushed a piece of hair out of my eyes.

"I'm sorry, honey," she said. "I know Miss Vest didn't mean to make you feel any worse off than you are."

"Then *why?*" I asked. "Why did she leave me here wishing for things I can't ever have?"

Twelve

When I heard the regulars down at Taggart's trading stories, I knew the drought must be even worse than I thought. I overheard Silas Hudgins say it had gotten so hot in Arkansas, corn kernels were exploding into popcorn right out in the field.

Then another man cut in, saying the fishing holes at Camp Rapidan had all gone dry. "Old Hoover might as well forget about catching any trout this summer," he went on. "He'd be better off staying in Washington anyhow, taking care of the sorry mess he's gotten this country into."

"What sorry mess?" I wanted to ask. I was standing at the counter, waiting to pay for a sack of flour and some spools of thread. But Mr. Taggart didn't even look at me as he took my money and pretty soon all the men were talking at once. So I pushed past their shoulders and elbows, leaving the buzz of their voices behind me.

I couldn't help feeling like a ghost again. With Mama and Daddy so caught up in when the next rain or the next paycheck was coming, I slipped in and out of the cabin without anyone noticing, like a puff of breeze or a shadow along the wall. But for once, I didn't mind being ignored. As soon as I finished chores every morning, I stole off through the woods for Aunt Birdy's, never stopping for breath until I was sitting on her front porch with my new boots laced and tied and the catalog resting in my lap.

At first I stayed on the front porch each morning, flipping through the catalog until my fingers turned black from the newsprint. Every so often I took little breaks to admire the fine fit of my boots as I stretched my legs out on the steps or walked along the railing, touching Aunt Birdy's stones. Aunt Birdy tried to leave me alone most of the time. She tinkered around the house, talking to herself and trying to nurse her roses and wisteria through the dry spell.

After a few days of studying, I managed to memorize the order of the catalog — hats and dresses were first, then corsets and gloves, then tires, guns, cookstoves, furniture, toys, baby buggies, and on and on. I turned to the end of the book, to the page full of houses. A new house for Mama — that would be number one on my wish list. I wanted the one Miss Vest had called a bungalow. The word sounded just like the house in the picture — neat and cozy with flower boxes under the windows, just right for three people.

I leaned down until my nose almost touched the page, squinting at the teensy print, but there were numbers and letters all mixed together. I knew enough to write down a *B* for bungalow, but what came after that? I rolled the pen back and forth between my sweaty fingers, waiting for something to make sense enough to write down. The empty square of paper gawked up at me.

It was too hard. Too hot to think out on the porch steps with the flat sky pressing down on me like a heavy hand. And whenever Aunt Birdy walked by, I kept imagining she was peering over my shoulder, checking to see if I had written anything yet.

"I'll be back after a while," I finally told her, gathering up my notepad and the catalog.

She gave me a funny look. I had never left before without changing back into my old boots or stacking up the presents from Miss Vest on the shelf by the fireplace.

"Where you going?" she asked.

"Not far."

I didn't know where I was going — just someplace cooler, where I could think. I headed for the trees, down an old deer path and across a drying creekbed, and pretty soon I found myself near the little graveyard where Riley and Grandpap Lockley were buried, over on the far side of the mountain near Big Meadows.

I knew Aunt Birdy visited all the time to put flowers on the graves, but I hadn't been there since Riley's funeral. It made me too sad to think of my brother buried in the ground with nothing but his initials chiseled on a piece of rock to show he had ever been alive. His whole life whittled down to those three little letters.

RJS
1921–1928

Mama had wanted to order a fancy marble headstone from the funeral parlor down in the valley. But there wasn't enough money, so Daddy had worked for days chiseling a slab of stone he found near our cabin.

When I came up on the worn path leading to the graveyard, I didn't stop. I walked all the way to the wrought-iron gate and stood with my hand on the latch. My new boots had scuffs on the toes, and the heels were mucky from crossing the creekbed, but beyond the gap, the cemetery looked so peaceful and shady. Even with the drought, the ground was still green with moss and periwinkle. Slowly, I pushed open the squeaky gate and headed for Riley's grave, winding my way through the stone slabs and whitewashed planks of wood that people had used for markers.

I smiled when I got to Riley's grave. Aunt Birdy had brought a bunch of black-eyed Susans and set them in a Mason jar by the headstone. I could see the same blaze of gold propped against Grandpap Lockley's stone down the hillside.

I kneeled in the periwinkle and set my catalog and notepad nearby. I remembered Aunt Birdy trying to convince me to visit the graveyard with her not long after the accident. She said she always talked to Grandpap Lockley and it made her feel better. But I still couldn't get the words to come. What would I say? Only "I'm sorry, Riley. I'm sorry."

I reached out and ran my hand over the letters Daddy had carved with the chisel. It was a shame he couldn't fit his whole name. Riley had been so proud of it. Even at four years old, he was already striking up conversations with complete strangers at Taggart's. Folks couldn't help reaching out to muss his hair and ask him what his name was and he would tell them in his loudest, most grown-up voice, "I'm Riley John Sloane. They named me after my grandpap. He's dead now." Mama would act embarrassed, but I knew deep inside she was pleased. She always gave him a little squeeze as she scooted him away.

He was so smart, so different from me. I picked up my catalog and turned to the bungalow page again. No matter how much I stared, the words still didn't come clear. I knew if Riley had gotten the chance to go to school, he would have been reading by now. But here I was, twelve years old, in the middle of a graveyard, still hopeless at reading.

A breeze blew up along the hillside and set the branches above me to rustling. The pages of the catalog fluttered, and I was just smoothing them out with my hand when something wet hit the newsprint. The drop of water landed right in the middle of the picture of the bungalow, blotting out the front door and one of the flower boxes. For a minute I thought it was a tear dripping down from my face. I had felt like crying all afternoon. But then . . . *splat*. Another wet spot landed, and another.

It was raining! Part of me wanted to laugh, to throw my head back and catch the drops on my tongue. But my catalog was getting wetter and the words were disappearing into the newsprint. I grabbed up my pen and the notepad and started writing as fast as I could, like a crazy person, copying all the words next to the bungalow picture.

I skipped over a string of numbers, then copied more words, trying to sound out the letters as I went along, as if I could catch them in my mouth before they disappeared. "S-s-s-s-suuuu-per-i-ooorrrrr," I said.

The sounds didn't make sense and the pages were getting limp. "C-c-c-c-on-st-st-st-rrrr-uuu-uc-tion."

But all at once, there it was. "Buh, Buh . . . Bun . . . Bung — Bunga . . . Bungalow!" I shouted. *"BUNGALOW!"*

I looked up at Riley's grave. "I did it, Riley," I whispered. "I read something." I glanced back at the word just to check, and it still made sense.

But the rain was falling harder now, splattering against my neck and soaking the back of my shirt. I pushed the catalog shut with the notepad inside and jumped to my feet, hugging the wet papers to my chest. Then I patted Riley's gravestone. "Thank you," I said.

I could see a patch of blue through the trees as I ran toward the gate. I knew the rain wouldn't amount to much more than a shower — probably only enough to rinse the brown layer of dust off the leaves. But for a while, even the drought didn't matter. I had the first word on my wish list and I could write it down now without even looking. *Bungalow.*

Thirteen

I wasn't expecting another miracle anytime soon. But just as the leaves were starting to flare up with color, Daddy came home with a heavy flour sack slung over his shoulder. When he heaved it to the floor and let Mama peek inside, she let out a gasp. "Chestnuts!" she cried. "Where on earth —"

Daddy laid open the bag for me to look, too. "We were over near Free Union, cutting down trees dying from blight to sell for pulpwood for making paper," he told us. "We'd been cutting all day and it was almost quitting time when we came over the ridge and ran into the biggest chestnut you ever seen, near six feet across. It was dead mostly, except for a couple old branches that still had all the leaves on 'em, and when you looked up, you could see they was just full of burrs with the nuts still inside, just hanging there . . . too high to reach."

While Daddy talked, I scooped up handfuls of the smooth brown nuts and let them rattle back down in the pile. They let off a smell that was dark and rich and reminded me of being little again, when it was my job to stomp on the stickery burrs until the chestnuts came free.

"How'd you get at the nuts, Daddy?" I asked, a little afraid of what his answer would be. "Did you have to cut the tree down?"

He shook his head. "Nope. It was way too big for the cross-saw. So we just stood there awhile, staring up at 'em, just hanging there . . . and then something happened."

"What?" Mama and I both asked at once.

Daddy smiled. "It rained."

"We didn't get any rain up here," Mama said.

"Well, it poured down at Free Union," Daddy went on. "So hard it knocked every one of them burrs down. Fell down on our heads like buckshot." He laughed his slow, deep laugh. "Good thing you packed me up that food in the flour sack, Alma. I got the most nuts, since I was the only one who had something to haul them home in."

Mama laughed, too, enough to smooth away the crease in her forehead and turn her face pretty again. "We'll take these down to Taggart's tomorrow. See how much he's paying per pound."

Daddy didn't say anything, and in the next breath, I found myself asking, "Can't we keep the chestnuts, Mama? And do like we used to?"

She looked from me to Daddy to the bag of nuts, then up at Daddy again. "But we need the money, Wes," she said and sighed.

He shrugged. "Why not, Alma? It'd be like old times."

"We can't be feeding everybody," Mama said. "We barely got enough to feed ourselves."

Daddy nodded. "We'll ask everybody to bring something to share."

Finally, Mama gave in and Daddy scrubbed his hand back and forth through my hair. We were going to have a chestnut roast, just like we used to.

Even though a few rain showers had fallen here and there, the drought wasn't over. But maybe it was that long, dry summer that made folks so willing to hike all the way over to Doubletop and forget about their worries for a while — because before we knew it, there were fifteen people coming to our cabin. Aunt Birdy invited everybody she saw until Mama begged her to stop. The Woodards were coming and the Hudginses and old Virgil Dawes with no teeth from the next hollow. I wasn't too happy about any of them, but I almost cried the morning of the roast when Aunt Birdy told me she had asked the Jessups, too.

"The Jessups?" I howled. "Why'd you do that?"

"I couldn't help it," Aunt Birdy said, dunking another drumstick in flour for the fried chicken we'd have that night. "I felt sorry for Preacher Jessup. He's been sitting in the back row at Sunday lessons ever since what happened when the Hoovers came to visit."

"Where does Dewey sit?"

"Right there in the back with his daddy. They slip in after Miss Vest has already started. Ida and her mother still sit up front, though. You know Ruby Jessup has always prided herself on her singing voice. And now with that marine from down at the camp playing piano ever' Sunday, she's not about to sit way in the back where nobody can hear her."

"What marine?"

"A tall, smiley fella. He's got a long, funny-sounding name, but I heard Miss Vest call him Wit. . . . I think he might be a little sweet on her."

I stood there with my mouth hanging open. I knew she was talking about Lou Witcofski. So much had happened since I had left school. Wit sweet on Miss Vest and playing the piano every Sunday? I would have given anything to see his fingers flying over the keys again, pounding out hymns.

"It's all Dewey's fault," I said.

"What do you mean?" Aunt Birdy asked me.

"If it wasn't for him starting the fight with Poke and them plowing into me and breaking my arm, I'd be there. I'd be there at school right now. I hate Dewey Jessup. He may be sitting in the back row, but at least he gets to be there to hear that piano every Sunday. . . . I hate him."

Aunt Birdy pointed her floury finger at me. "Hate is a mighty powerful thing, Apry. If you're not careful, it'll eat you inside out." She reached for another drumstick. "You're so busy hating Dewey, I guess you don't even want to hear who else I invited to the chestnut roast."

"All right," I said, trying to look sorry. "Who?"

Aunt Birdy glanced over her shoulder. Mama and Daddy were still outside setting planks across sawhorses for the tables. "Miss Vest," she whispered.

"Miss Vest!" I felt my face breaking into a smile. "What did Mama say?"

Aunt Birdy flinched. "Shh. I haven't told

her yet," she said. "I'm waiting for the right time. Maybe after I get this chicken fried . . ."

Fourteen

With all the house cleaning and biscuit cutting and gravy stirring, the right time for Aunt Birdy to confess what she had done never came. So it was a complete shock to Mama when Miss Vest appeared, riding up in the Jessups' wagon with an apple pie perched on her lap. I saw Mama's face go white, and she grabbed Aunt Birdy's elbow in a claw-hold. "What did you do?" she asked, gritting her teeth.

But Aunt Birdy was already off the porch, hurrying out to greet everyone, to make a fuss over Mrs. Jessup's big pot of turnip greens and Miss Vest's apple pie. I stood in the doorway, holding my breath, afraid of what Mama might do next. Somehow, though, she found a way to collect herself by the time Miss Vest came up on the porch to say hello. I stepped back in the shadows to listen.

"I wanted to thank you for inviting me today," I heard Miss Vest say.

Mama was quiet. Then she said, "April's not coming back to school, Miss Vest, if that's what you're thinking."

Miss Vest dropped her voice down low. "I know how you feel, Mrs. Sloane, and as much as I disagree with you, I want you to know I didn't come here today to try and talk you or your daughter into anything. Mainly, I just came to see how April's doing."

At that point I should have stepped out of the doorway. And I wanted to. More than anything, I wanted to run to Miss Vest and hug her, but for some reason I couldn't. There was so much I needed to tell her — about the catalog and the spot by Riley's grave where I studied now and how much I loved my new boots. And I wanted to ask her about Kentucky and if all her daddy's tobacco plants had dried up over the summer and what the kids at school were working on now.

But it was just too much with Mama and all the other folks there. So I slipped back farther behind the door and waited until Miss Vest had moved away.

For the rest of the night, I stayed busy running back and forth to the kitchen to wash another stack of plates or heat up the food folks had brought. Miss Vest kept trying to catch my eye, but when it was time to eat, Ida and Luella raced for the spots on the bench next to her and talked her ear off all the way through supper. When I passed Miss Vest a plate of food, she couldn't do much more than look up at me and smile.

Then Daddy called me over to the corner of the yard to help get the chestnuts ready. While he carved X marks in the shells and stoked up the fire in a pit he had dug in the ground, I divvied up the nuts into tin pie plates. Then we both squatted down and held our pans over the flames with the tongs Mama had made out of heavy fencing wire.

Soon it was getting dark and chilly, and folks started drifting over, pulled by the sweet smell of the roasting nuts and the warmth of the fire. Ida came over with Little Elton on her hip. She set him down in the dirt so she and Luella could help themselves to some of the cooled nuts. I hadn't seen them since the springtime, but they didn't even bother saying "Hello" or "Thank you" or "Where you been?" as I held out the pan. They peeled open the chestnuts with their teeth and bit out the creamy insides, ignoring me and Little Elton, who was fussing to be picked up again. Finally, Ida yanked her brother off his wobbly feet and handed him to Dewey, who had just come wandering over.

"Here," she said. "You take him."

"Where's Ma?" Dewey asked.

"I don't know," Ida snapped, "but it's your turn." Then she and Luella flounced off.

I listened to Little Elton whining until I couldn't stand it anymore. I knew what to do. I ran inside the cabin for a jar of sorghum and some feathers from the pillow on Mama and Daddy's bed.

Then I marched back outside and grabbed Little Elton out of Dewey's arms. "Here," I said, handing Dewey the jar of sorghum. "Open that."

Dewey stared at me like I was crazy. "Why?" he asked.

"Just open it."

Once Dewey had pried off the lid, I took the jar and dipped Little Elton's fingers into the thick syrup, then pushed some feathers into his chubby hands. In the next minute he stopped crying and fell into a daze with his little mouth frozen in a round O as he tried to pull the sticky feathers off his fingers. I sat down on a log near the fire with him on my lap. When he had finished pulling the feathers off one hand, he set to work on the other.

Dewey stood beside us, watching. "That's a pretty good trick," he said. "Where'd you learn that?"

"Mama taught me," I said. "When Riley was little."

Dewey fell quiet for a minute, then he said, "Your arm's healed up. When you think you're coming back to school?"

I glanced up at him. "You sure are full of questions."

Dewey shrugged. "So, when you coming back?"

"Never," I told him.

His eyebrows pulled together. "Never? What do you mean 'never'?"

I looked down at the glowing fire, trying to think of what to say, but before I could answer, Mama came bearing down on us. "April Sloane, what in creation are you doing?" she said. "Ruby Jessup doesn't want Little Elliott covered in sorghum on their way home. Go on inside and fetch a wet washrag."

"Yes, ma'am," I said. I stood up and Dewey took Little Elton. He looked sorry for me, like he wanted to say something, but I hurried off before he had the chance. It was foolish of me to have thought the chestnut roast would be any fun. Seeing Dewey and the other folks talking and cracking chestnuts around the kerosene lamp at the table just made me feel more alone. At least Mama had decided to join them. As I walked by, I saw her slide onto the bench next to Daddy.

I pushed open the door of the cabin and was heading for the wash bucket around the corner in the kitchen when I ran smack into Miss Vest. She was holding a stack of dirty plates.

"April!" she cried, setting the dishes on the wooden sideboard with a clatter. "There you are!" She reached out and laid her hands on my shoulders. "I thought I'd never get to talk to you tonight. How have you been? How's your arm?"

I was so happy to be with her again I could barely come up with the words to answer. "Fine," I said finally. "My arm's coming along." I bent and straightened it a few times so she could see. Then I stood there grinning while she gazed around the front room. I had forgotten she had never been inside before, since Mama refused to open the door when she had knocked. All of a sudden, I felt ashamed of how plain and homely our cabin must have looked compared with the schoolhouse. The only thing worth admiring was the stack of oak-split baskets sitting by the fireplace.

"Mama made those," I said, following Miss Vest's eye.

"They're beautiful. . . . Is that where you

sleep?" she asked, nodding to the lumpy bed.

"Naw. That's Mama and Daddy's. I sleep upstairs in the loft."

Miss Vest walked over to the far side of the room and peered up the thick wooden ladder that led through a dark hole in the ceiling. "Up there?"

I nodded. "Wanna see?"

Her face sparked up. "I'd love to."

I grabbed the kerosene lamp off the table and the next thing I knew, Miss Vest was climbing up the creaky ladder behind me. At the top, I held out the lantern so she could see. Then I scrambled over and yanked the quilt straight on my straw tick, wishing my bed was resting on a frame instead of across the cold, splintery floorboards.

Once Miss Vest climbed through the opening, she had to stoop so her head wouldn't hit the rafters. "Whew," she breathed, smoothing out her skirt. "I should have dressed better for climbing."

"You can sit here," I said shyly, patting the bed beside me. Miss Vest hunched her way over and plopped down on the mattress. I couldn't help laughing at the way she was huffing for breath, still trying to keep her skirt tucked over her knees.

Then Miss Vest broke up laughing, too. She threw herself back on my bed, letting her legs sprawl out and her arms go limp like she had just finished climbing Old Rag. I dropped back beside her, still giggling, and for a minute we both stared up, watching the light from the lamp flicker over the rafters.

Then Miss Vest pointed to a crack in the slanted roof above us, where you could just make out thin slivers of night sky through the boards. "April! Don't you just freeze up here in the winter with the wind whistling through?"

"It's not so bad," I said. "When it gets real cold, I sleep downstairs. Daddy needs to patch the roof with tarpaper again. That makes it warmer." I didn't tell her about when it snowed, how the flakes sifted down on my quilt like flour.

Miss Vest cocked her head back, squinting closer at the boards. Then she rolled over on her stomach and stopped. "What's that?"

She had seen them. The rolled-up pieces of paper I had lodged into the cracks near my pillow. Miss Vest sat up and reached for the lamp beside the bed. She held it up, letting the light slide across the boards. I hadn't realized until then how many slips of paper I had curled and stuffed into every nook and cranny. There were lots of them. A whole summer's worth.

"Those are my wish lists," I said softly.

She turned to look at me. "You mean you really made them?" she asked. "Can I see?"

I could feel myself blushing as I leaned across her and pulled the closest roll of paper from the wall. I gave it to her, and she set the lamp at her feet and smoothed out the strip of paper on her knee.

"April," she whispered, "you did this on your own? *Look*. 'Fur Collar. Cuffs. Cast-Iron Range. Christmas Tree Tinsel.' . . . Can you really read these?"

"Uh-huh. I worked on them every day this summer, and this fall, too." I reached for another list and unrolled it on the bed. "Here's one I made with prices." I followed the words with my finger and slowly said them out loud, "Jewel Box . . . one dollar ninety-eight cents. . . . Lace Drapes . . . three dollars. . . . All-Silk Umbrella . . . five dollars ninety-five cents."

Miss Vest listened with her mouth open, and I wanted to burst with how proud I felt each time she pulled down a new list from the wall. There were all kinds of lists — some with only *B* things like "Bungalow" and "Butterfly Book" and "Baby Buggy" and others with just *K* or *L* words. Some were dream lists for Aunt Birdy and some for Daddy. On one list I had written down "Rain Bonnet," then changed my mind and erased "Bonnet," thinking how nice it would be just to have the Rain. I waited for Miss Vest to get tired of hearing me read, but she just kept pulling the lists down until we had a whole pile of curly papers in the middle of the bed.

There were only a few lists left in the cracks when she handed me one that I didn't want her to see. But before I could sneak it into the pile, she leaned over to find out what had made me turn quiet.

"You only wrote one word on that one," Miss Vest said, peering over my shoulder. "Phonograph. But why'd you cross it out? Did you decide you don't want a phonograph after all?"

"I don't know why I wrote that," I mumbled. "Anyhow, we used to have one."

Miss Vest looked surprised. "You had a phonograph?"

I nodded. "A Victrola. I reckon I saw the picture in the catalog and it got me thinking. . . . But I wouldn't want another one."

"Why not? What happened to it?"

I stared down at the smudged letters on

160

the scrap of paper in my lap. "We sold it to the Jessups," I said finally. "When Riley died. He was crazy about that Victrola and seeing it sit there quiet day after day just reminded Mama too much. So Daddy sold it."

Miss Vest reached over and took my hand. "I'm sorry," she said. We sat for a while without saying anything, and I didn't take my hand away. Then Miss Vest smiled and started to push herself up from the bed. "We'd better get down to the party."

"It was playing when it happened," I whispered.

Miss Vest turned around. "What'd you say, April?"

I swallowed hard. "You know that song 'Let Me Call You Sweetheart'?"

Miss Vest sat down again. "Yes."

"That was the one playing."

My heart fluttered up in my chest. I hadn't meant to tell. I had never told anyone before. But somehow before I could stop myself, Miss Vest was nodding and holding my hand again and I was saying more. "That was our favorite song. Riley and me used to play it over and over again when Mama and Daddy weren't home. We were trying to learn how to waltz, like they had showed us once. We wanted to surprise

161

Mama. But that night, the night it happened, Riley was tired and wanted to stop,
but I didn't want to, not until we got it perfect. So I just kept cranking up the Victrola
and pulling him around the room."

I squeezed my eyes shut. When I opened
them, everything was blurry with tears like I
was looking at Miss Vest through a piece of
thick glass. "Riley started whining a little
and it made me mad. I remember saying,
'Don't you want to surprise Mama? You're
her favorite, aren't you? Aren't you her favorite?' " I swiped the tears out of my eyes.
"Wasn't that an awful thing to say to a little
boy, Miss Vest?"

"April, we all say things we don't mean
when we're angry."

I closed my eyes again and shook my head
back and forth. "I was dancing him around
so fast, I didn't even see it happen. . . . But
we must have moved too close to the fire
and his nightshirt caught —"

I heard Miss Vest suck in her breath. She
squeezed my hand tighter.

"And all of a sudden, it was on fire. And I
just froze. . . . *I just stood there.* . . . I was too
scared to run for water or push him out in
the snow, and he was tearing around the
room."

"Oh, April," Miss Vest whispered. For a

162

minute I sank against her, letting the tears drip down. She rocked me back and forth a little and said, "Shh, shh." Finally, I reached up to wipe my nose with the back of my hand and all at once, I remembered Little Elton's washrag and all the people downstairs.

I jerked up straight. "Miss Vest," I said in a panic, *"you can't ever tell Mama.* She and Daddy don't know. I told them Riley got burned when I was out fetching wood . . . and — and all this time, they believed me. They figure Riley was playing in the fire or something, but that's not true. He never would have done that. . . . *Never.* He knew better. But I can't tell Mama it was all my fault. I can't —"

But Miss Vest wasn't even looking at me. She was looking over my shoulder. Then I heard the creak. When I turned around, Mama was standing on the ladder, staring at us, with just her head and shoulders poking through the opening to the loft. She climbed another step, rising up just like the genie from the bottle in Miss Vest's book of fairy tales.

Then she stopped. Even in the shadows, I could see the hurt burning in her eyes. "You don't need to tell me nothing, either one of you. I heard it all."

Her voice was shaking. I could see it took all her strength just to hang on to the ladder and keep from screaming at us.

Miss Vest tried to push herself up from my bed. "Mrs. Sloane —"

But as soon as Miss Vest spoke, Mama let go. "All this time, April, you been lying to me!" she shrieked, dragging herself up into the loft. "If it weren't for you, he'd still be here!"

Miss Vest stepped in front of Mama, blocking her from bearing down on me. "Mrs. Sloane!" she cried. "It was an accident, a terrible accident, but April —"

Mama turned on her, her face twisting with fury. "*Get away from me!* You think you know everything there is to know about April, don't you? All this time you been wanting her back at school so bad. *Well, go ahead, then!* You got what you came for, didn't you? Take her with you when you go. I can't stand the sight of her anymore."

Then without giving me another look, Mama disappeared down the ladder, leaving her words splitting through the air.

I stayed huddled up on my bed while Miss Vest hurried down to try and make things right again. I could hear the front door squeaking open and closed, then all the guests saying their goodbyes. Later I could hear Miss Vest's gentle voice humming on and on, then Daddy's and Aunt Birdy's voices, all coaxing and pleading with Mama to please, please come to her senses. I leaned forward, listening hard for Mama's answer, but there wasn't one word from her, not one.

I could picture her sitting at the table in the kitchen with her hands locked in a fist in her lap and her face full of bitterness. She was probably staring across at the fireplace in the front room, going over in her head what I had done to Riley.

After a while, I couldn't stand the waiting anymore. I packed my clothes and my wish lists into a bundle and climbed down the ladder. Aunt Birdy and Daddy and Miss Vest were standing around Mama, who was leaning into the sideboard scrubbing at the wood with a rag even though it was probably already clean. They all stopped when they saw me, and Mama turned. But I let my eyes brush past her hard stare. Then I walked outside and headed toward the fire pit where we had roasted the chestnuts.

It didn't take more than a minute for my wish lists to catch on the coals and burn down to ash. By the time Aunt Birdy came scurrying outside to find me, they were gone. I pretended to be warming my hands over the fire.

She stood beside me for a little bit, staring into the coals. "Why didn't you tell me, Apry?" she finally asked. "Why'd you keep such a thing locked up inside all this time?"

"It was all my fault. I didn't think you could forgive me if you knew the truth."

Aunt Birdy put her arm around my shoulders. "There's no forgiving to it, honey. It was an accident, plain and simple. You never meant for such an awful thing to happen. We all know how much you loved Riley."

I turned and buried my head in her old wool sweater. She wrapped her little arms around me and held on tight.

"Apry, honey, why don't you come stay with me till your mama's thinking clearer?"

I shook my head against her shoulder, trying not to start crying again. "Miss Vest says I can stay with her for a while."

"But you should be with your kin right now, Apry."

I sighed and pulled away. "She'd hold it against you if you take me in, Aunt Birdy. I'll just stay with Miss Vest for now till Mama . . . till she changes her mind."

Daddy couldn't make things right, either. "It won't be long, April," he said after joining me by the fire. "I bet your mama's gonna wake up tomorrow and be ready to talk this out. . . ."

I didn't hear the rest of what he said. All I could think of was his lady's-slipper story, about the little Indian girl lost forever in the snow. Daddy's eyes looked so sad. Would I be his Indian girl?

In the end, there was nothing for him to do but hitch up the wagon and drive me and Miss Vest to the schoolhouse in the dark. He helped me carry my things to the yellow room at the top of the stairs. I sat down on the bed, feeling numb all over. Then Daddy kissed me on the top of the head and told me he and Mama would come back for me soon.

1932

Fifteen

One Sunday, not long after my fourteenth birthday, we had a flag-raising ceremony at the schoolhouse. Mr. Jessup had put in a new flagpole out front overlooking the valley, and for weeks Wit had been helping our class learn the national anthem and some other patriotic songs to sing for the congregation once we raised the flag.

Everybody's parents were there but mine. A year before, I might have searched the crowd, praying to see Mama or Daddy somewhere in the wall of faces. "Today's the day," I told myself at every school function. "Today's the day they'll come to take me home." But I had given up hoping months ago — after the first Christmas passed without a word, then my thirteenth birthday, then the second Christmas.

Miss Vest and Aunt Birdy were my family now. Aunt Birdy never missed a chance to come to the schoolhouse. For the flag raising, she was wearing a little blue straw hat that I had never seen before. Even though it was old and had a sprig of tired silk daisies drooping off one side, the color brought out the blue in her eyes.

"So you're gonna be the one to raise the flag, Apry?" she asked me as we stood waiting for the ceremony to start. "How come you get to do it?"

"The kids in the class voted and picked me," I told her, trying not to smile too wide.

"They did?" She gasped. "All of 'em voted for you? Even *you know who?*"

She looked over her shoulder for Ida and Luella. I had told her how much they despised me for living in the schoolhouse with Miss Vest. Then, as if that wasn't enough to make them jealous, Miss Vest had cut my hair in a bob like hers and started making me dresses on her sewing machine.

"Shh," I said. "I know *they* didn't vote for me. It was the little kids, mainly." Now that I could read and write without stumbling over words, Miss Vest sometimes asked me to work with the younger ones on their lessons. Whenever they were having trouble, I pulled out the Sears, Roebuck and helped them start on their own wish lists, until pretty soon they were begging for more time with me and the catalog.

"What about Dewey? Who'd he vote for?"

I laughed. "Himself, probably." The truth was Dewey and I had been getting along fine ever since I had wandered into the schoolroom one night and found Miss Vest giving Preacher Jessup reading lessons. I couldn't believe it. *Preacher Jessup* sitting at a desk three sizes too small and struggling over a story about Henny Penny and Clucky Lucky. When Dewey came to fetch his pa and found me listening at the doorway to the classroom, I could tell we had a bargain just from the look in his eyes. If I didn't tell anybody about his daddy, Dewey would leave me alone.

Aunt Birdy broke into a sad little smile. I had grown a couple inches over the last year, and she had to tilt her head back to look at me. "You're getting so big, Apry. Your mama wouldn't even recognize you now if she passed you on the road."

I didn't answer. Aunt Birdy knew I didn't like her reminding me, but sometimes she couldn't help herself.

"She'd be so proud of you today," she went on, gazing down on the valley. "You know she named you for the month of April not just 'cause that's when you were born. April was always your mother's favorite time —"

"*Please,* Aunt Birdy," I said, trying to keep my voice down. I didn't want to hear it. Wit was hurrying toward me with the new flag folded in its neat triangle, and all the kids were lining up around Miss Vest.

Aunt Birdy perked up when she saw Wit. He kissed her on the cheek, then handed me the flag. "You about ready?" he asked.

I nodded and followed him to the front of the crowd. Soon Miss Vest was calling for quiet, and we all bowed our heads while she led us in a prayer.

"We've come today," Miss Vest said, "to ask for God's help in guiding our country through these times of hardship. We ask you, Lord, to give our president strength in the face of this Depression, with its many challenges. . . ."

I still didn't really understand what Miss Vest meant by the word "Depression." Most families I knew seemed to be doing better than ever. The drought had ended the spring before, and a lot of men had found good-paying jobs building the new highway that was supposed to run along the crest of the mountains all the way from Thornton to Swift Run Gap. Aunt Birdy had heard that Daddy got a job on the road crew. And even though I pretended not to listen when she told me, I couldn't help thinking of him whenever I heard the rumble of trucks and bulldozers off in the distance. Daddy. He never came like he promised, and there was only one explanation: he couldn't forgive me, either.

"April?" Miss Vest called.

I jumped. Everybody was watching me. I hurried to my spot, and Miss Vest helped me unfold the flag the way we had practiced. Then I hooked it on the metal clips and reached for the rope. I felt the old pain in my arm as soon as I started to pull the flag up toward the bright blue sky. It didn't surprise me anymore. I had gotten used to feeling an ache whenever I swept the kitchen floor or carried a bucket of water. The last thing I wanted to do was complain to Miss Vest, especially after all that she was doing — feeding and clothing me, letting me stay in the beautiful spare bedroom so long that she didn't call it the guest quarters anymore. It was "April's room" now.

Still, I wished Mr. Jessup had oiled the pulleys a little better. It seemed to take forever to yank the flag to the top. But finally I was done, and everyone clapped as the flag caught the breeze. Then we put our hands on our hearts and sang the first three verses of "America the Beautiful."

After the ceremony, when everybody was heading back to the schoolhouse for cupcakes and punch, Wit came up to me with a sly look on his face. "So, Miss April," he said, "I thought you'd be happy about being elected the Queen of Flag Raising."

" 'Course I'm happy," I said.

Wit leaned toward me as he walked. "Then why'd you look like you were chewing tacks the whole time you were pulling on that rope?"

"What do you mean?" I asked, trying to turn my face away.

"You know what I mean, April," Wit said, putting his hand on my shoulder to stop me as I tried to scoot up the schoolhouse steps behind the other kids. "How long has your arm been hurting?"

I glared at him. I loved Wit, with his long arms and legs and his funny stories and lively songs. Whenever he showed up at the schoolhouse to give us a music lesson, all the kids cheered. But he had been dropping by too much lately, showing up after school hours and calling Miss Vest by her first name — Christine. Most of the time Wit invited me to come along on their strolls through the woods or their picnics at Big Meadows. But once in a while he didn't, and I couldn't help feeling pangs of meanness cut through me, like hot knives in butter.

Miss Vest breezed up beside us. "You did

a wonderful job, April." Then she looked at me closer. "What's wrong?"

"I think the Flag Queen isn't telling us something," Wit said. He held up one hand with his big palm facing out. "Here, April, push against me with your left hand, as hard as you can."

"Why?" I asked, starting to turn red. Aunt Birdy had come hurrying over, too, to see what all the fuss was about.

"Just push," Wit said again.

I put my palm up to his and gave a little shove.

"You can do better than that."

I let out a long sigh and pushed at him harder, feeling my blood start to boil. Why did he always have to be butting in, nosing around in my business?

Wit pushed back, making me even madder, so mad that I winced before I could stop myself.

"Ow!" I yelped, rubbing at the sore spot on my arm.

Miss Vest stepped toward me. "April, isn't that the arm you broke? You mean to tell me it's been hurting you all this time?"

"Maybe just a little," I murmured, looking at the ground.

"I knew it. I knew it," Aunt Birdy huffed, shaking her head back and forth.

"Why didn't you tell me?" Miss Vest asked.

"She didn't want to worry you, I imagine," Wit cut in. He patted my shoulder and I held myself back from shrugging his hand away.

"Well, tell you what," he went on. "The Hoovers will be at camp next weekend, and Dr. Boone, the president's physician, always comes with them. I'll tell him about April. Maybe he can take a look at her arm on Saturday and help us decide what to do."

Miss Vest nodded. "All right," she said. "If you can set it up, we'll come over on Saturday." I lifted my head up and stared. I couldn't believe the two of them, talking about going to Camp Rapidan like it was nothing special, like we were just going on another one of their silly picnics.

Sixteen

I was so restless the next week waiting for my trip to Camp Rapidan, even Aunt Birdy got tired of me. "You're making me nervous with all that moving around. You're like a fried egg in a greased pan," she said, shooing me out the front door. "Now get."

For three years I had been dreaming of Camp Rapidan and imagining a grand country estate rising up from a clearing in the woods. The newspapers even called it "the Summer White House." So I couldn't help being disappointed when Saturday finally came and I walked through the front gates and saw nothing but plain pine-board cabins hidden among the trees.

"Is this it?" I wanted to ask Miss Vest. But I kept my mouth shut, and it turned out that the farther we walked, the more I liked what I saw. Every time we turned a corner on one of the twisty dirt pathways, there was something special waiting — a little bridge over a winding stream, a fern garden, a circle of logs for sitting around an outdoor fireplace, or a pit for throwing horseshoes.

The paths were lined with stones and mountain laurel bushes drooping with pink and white blossoms. It was hard to believe these were the same ordinary woods Riley and I used to run through a few years ago. Now they seemed magic and full of surprises — especially with the strange man leading Miss Vest and me along.

I leaned toward Miss Vest. "Who's he?" I whispered. I had never seen him before. He wore a heavy blue suit that made him look stiff and out of place in the middle of the woods.

Miss Vest gave me a mysterious look. "He's Secret Service."

"What's that?" I asked, feeling my eyes get round. *Secret Service.* Whatever it was sounded dark and dangerous.

Miss Vest smiled. "Don't worry," she said in a low voice. "That just means he's here to protect the president. Anywhere the Hoovers go, they have to have an agent following, just in case there's ever any trouble. When I went riding with Mrs. Hoover last fall, one of them had to ride along behind us. I felt sorry for him. I don't think he had ever been on a horse before in his life."

The Secret Service man turned around. For a minute I thought he was going to fuss at us for whispering, then he pointed toward a cabin through the trees. It was one of the larger ones, with a giant stone chimney built up the side.

"Here's the president's cabin," he said. "Mrs. Hoover is waiting for you out on the terrace. She wanted you to stop by and see her before you meet with Dr. Boone."

Miss Vest knew the way. She thanked the Secret Service man, then led me up on the wide sitting porch that wrapped around the cabin. I had never seen another porch like it. There was no roof, and huge hemlock trees were growing through holes cut into the floor. We walked around the corner and saw Mrs. Hoover, sitting on a cushioned chair, knitting and looking out on the fork of two creeks tumbling down the rocky mountainside.

"There you are," she said, looking up from her knitting. She patted the chair beside her. "Sit right here by me, April."

Over the past year, Mrs. Hoover had visited the schoolhouse enough times to make us all forget to be nervous around her. Sometimes she brought lunch for the class in big wicker hampers and ate sandwiches and cookies with us outside under the trees. After a while, I started noticing little things that made her seem more like a friendly neighbor than the first lady — like the little space that showed between her front teeth when she smiled or the way her hairpins came loose from the silver braid wrapped around her head.

I knew Miss Vest had probably told Mrs. Hoover about me a long time ago, all about Riley and about Mama sending me away. At first I was ashamed. But the more I got to know Mrs. Hoover, the less I minded what she knew.

A little man in a short white jacket came out from the cabin with a pitcher of lemonade and three tall glasses full of ice cubes on a tray. Mrs. Hoover poured me a drink, and I took a sip, trying to stop myself from gulping the whole thing down at once. While Miss Vest and Mrs. Hoover talked, I held my glass in my lap and looked around, trying to soak everything in — the smell of petunias in the big flowerpots around the porch and the roar of the water rushing over the rocks.

Mrs. Hoover was leaning toward Miss Vest. "Now, Christine," I heard her say, "when Mr. Hoover joins us, make sure to tell him some of your wonderful stories about the children. They always make him laugh, and he certainly could use a little diversion with this election coming up."

The election. I knew Miss Vest had been

worried about that, too. There were only six more months till the country had to vote whether to keep Mr. Hoover for another term or throw him out and pick a new president. Every morning around breakfast time, someone from the marine camp delivered a copy of the *Washington Post.* Miss Vest read the front page each day and sighed, barely even glancing up at me as she chewed her toast.

Sometimes, after she had headed into the schoolroom, I tried to make sense of the headlines. "Hoover Policies Face Mounting Criticism" . . . "Protest Marchers Gather at Steps of White House" . . . It wasn't hard to see things weren't going the best for the president. One cartoon drawing I saw showed him standing over a crowd of people who were reaching out their arms and crying for help. But President Hoover had his hands over his ears in the cartoon and was saying, "Sorry, I can't hear you."

I couldn't understand it. Herbert Hoover was the one who had built our school and sent us books and presents and truckloads of flour and sugar when the drought was so bad. How could people think he was mean and no good?

Mrs. Hoover looked up from her knitting. "Weegie!" she said as a big black dog with pointed ears ran up the porch steps. He trotted over to her and pushed his long nose into her lap. Mrs. Hoover scratched him behind the ears.

Just then two men came around the corner. "Here they are," Mrs. Hoover said. "I knew if Weegie was here, they couldn't be far behind."

"How was the fishing, Joel?" she called out.

"We got a few bites," the man said, setting his pole against the side of the cabin. "But the president wasn't in the mood for biding his time."

"Oh, dear," Mrs. Hoover said. "Well, never mind. Come have some lemonade and meet your new patient."

Dr. Boone walked over and introduced himself, but I barely heard a word he said. I was busy watching the man behind him. I knew it was the president, but he looked so tired and pale, so different from the steady-eyed man in the portrait at the schoolhouse who calmly guarded over us every day. There were deep lines around his mouth and eyes and his hair seemed thinner and grayer. It was hard not to stare.

"Can't you sit down and join us, Bert?" Mrs. Hoover asked. "Miss Vest was just telling me a wonderful story about the barbershop she's opened."

"A barbershop, eh?" Dr. Boone asked, sneaking a worried glance at the president.

Miss Vest smiled. "That's right. When I cut April's hair last year, all the other girls started asking me to bob their hair, too. But I was a little nervous about cutting off all those braids and getting into trouble with the girls' parents, so I've limited my business to boys. They sit on an old chestnut stump in the yard behind the schoolhouse and I go to work. . . ."

Her voice trailed off. The president wasn't listening. He was still jingling the coins in his pocket, gazing out toward the creek.

"Bert, dear," Mrs. Hoover said, "Christine was trying to tell you —"

The president gave himself a little shake. "Oh, of course, of course. I'm sorry, Miss Vest. . . . How's Mr. Jessup doing? Has he decided to go back to his preaching yet?"

"I'm afraid not," Miss Vest said. "He *still* doesn't think he's ready, even though he's been coming for lessons in the evenings for almost two years now. He's just about worked his way through the whole Bible."

"I met him the other day out riding," Mrs. Hoover said. "He told me he can't wait to cast his vote in November."

President Hoover raised his eyebrows. "Oh, really? Who's he going to vote for?"

"Bert!" Mrs. Hoover scolded.

"Well, Lou, you never know. Loyalty's a hard thing to come by these days." He forced out a hard little laugh. Then, before anybody could change the subject, he told us he had to go back to his office and get some more work done.

After he had gone, Mrs. Hoover turned to Dr. Boone and said under her breath, "Joel, can't you get him to take a rest this afternoon?"

"I'll see what I can do," Dr. Boone told her quietly, then he spun around to face me and clapped his hands. "*Now,* young lady, what's this I hear about a sore arm?"

Somehow Dewey found out I was going to Washington, D.C., with Miss Vest to have my arm fixed. Ever since I had moved into the schoolhouse, we had been getting along fine. I never told anyone about his father's late-night reading lessons, and Dewey never dared to call me names or whistle the old Victrola songs anymore. But my trip to Washington must have set him off again. One day at recess he cornered me while I was eating my lunch on the bench by the new flagpole.

"So I suppose you're gonna get to visit the White House, too?" Dewey asked with his mouth all twisted to one side.

"Probably not," I lied. I pulled an apple from my lunch pail and pretended to be busy polishing it on the hem of my skirt. "Miss Vest says we won't have much time before we have to get to the hospital."

Dewey crossed his arms over his chest. "I reckon you ought to be thanking me for breaking that arm of yours."

I started to take a bite of my apple, then froze, letting my mouth drop open wider. "*Thanking* you?"

"That's right," he said. "You know your broken arm's the only reason you got to go to Camp Rapidan and now Washington, D.C. — and probably the only reason you got to move into the schoolhouse when your mother kicked you out. Mama says Miss Vest felt like it was all her fault and she felt like she *had* to take you in."

Dewey started to turn away.

But it was too late. I flung my apple back in my lunch pail, so hard that it clunked against the metal bottom. "Well, maybe you're right, Dewey," I said. I stood up and brushed the crumbs off my skirt. "Maybe I should thank you. I wasn't going to say so at first, but come to think of it, I'd break two or three more bones to pay for all the fun I'm gonna have in Washington. Miss Vest ordered me a new dress and a hat and my own pocketbook for the trip, and we're gonna ride the train from Charlottesville and stay in a fancy hotel and go see all the museums, and then we're gonna have lunch at the White House —"

"Shoot," Dewey spit back. "I wouldn't eat horse feed with those Hoovers."

"What are you talking about? You're the possum boy, remember? You've always fallen all over yourself trying to make friends with the Hoovers."

Dewey shook his head. "Not anymore. Not after what they got planned for us."

I rolled my eyes and acted like I was getting ready to walk away.

Dewey squinted at me harder. "You haven't heard, have you?" he said. "I bet you don't even know why they're making that new road across the mountain."

" 'Course I do. Paved roads are better than dirt ones."

Dewey snorted. "You don't know nothing," he said. "I'll tell you why they're building that road. President Hoover and his men are planning to make a big park right here — right where we're standing." He jabbed his finger toward the ground.

Now I was the one crossing my arms. "What do you mean, a park? What kind of park?"

Dewey was almost shouting now. "I mean the kind of place where city folks come with their cars and their blankets and their camping tents. They'll be driving all over creation, nosing around and taking pictures, trying to get away from the city."

"Where'd you hear that?" I said, letting my voice fill up with disgust.

"Everybody knows it. They're all talking about it down at Taggart's. Mr. Taggart says we ought to be getting ready to fight, because the government's gonna try to move us off our land — just because they gotta make room for a park."

"I don't believe a word you say," I said through my teeth.

Dewey put on a high, singsong voice. " 'I don't believe a word you say,' " he mocked. "Well, Miss Priss, if you're so sure of yourself, why don't you just ask those Hoovers for yourself. You're gonna be right there in the White House next week. You ask them — ask them if it ain't true they're gonna try to move us out and put a park on our land."

"I *will* ask them," I snapped back. "Don't you worry. I'll ask them first chance I get."

Seventeen

"Where to?" the driver grunted once he had loaded our suitcases in the back of the bright yellow taxicab and climbed behind the steering wheel.

Miss Vest winked at me. "The White House, please," she sang out.

I could see the driver's face in the little mirror up front. He raised one eyebrow. "You want the White House, ma'am?"

"That's right," Miss Vest said. "But not the front entrance. We'd like the north portico, please."

This time the driver turned around in his seat to give us a hard look. "The north portico, huh?"

Miss Vest nodded. Finally, the driver shrugged and steered out into traffic, mumbling, "Whatever you say, ma'am."

I leaned back against the leather seat and closed my eyes. My whole body felt wobbly and my head was whirling so hard I had to remind myself to take slow, deep breaths. Miss Vest had warned me — about the honking horns and the crowds of people and the tall buildings. Before our trip, she had gone through the guidebook with me page by page. But no amount of explaining could have prepared me for it — the train barreling along like a thunderstorm and the blur of farms and fields turning into acres of houses, one on top of the other.

Then there was the strange town of shacks we rode through right before we pulled into Union Station. Some of the shacks were made of cardboard and old rusted pieces of tin, and as we rumbled by, I caught sight of a group of scrawny kids cooking something on a stick over an open fire.

"What was *that* place?" I asked Miss Vest as I looked back over my shoulder. One of the little girls had broken away from the fire and was hopping up and down, waving at the train.

The man in the seat behind me spoke up. "That was Hooverville, honey."

When the man had gone back to reading his newspaper, Miss Vest leaned over and said, "You know that place wasn't really called Hooverville, right, April? He just said that because poor folks live there and some people think it's the president's fault that they're out of jobs and proper homes."

I nodded. *"Out of proper homes,"* she had

said. All at once, I remembered my fight with Dewey. According to him, we'd be living in cardboard shacks, too, once the Hoovers and the government got finished with us. But I was sure it was all a big lie, and first chance I got, I'd ask Mrs. Hoover myself and she would tell me so.

As we rode along in the taxicab, I took another deep breath, trying to push Dewey out of my mind. Miss Vest must have heard me sigh. She reached over and squeezed my hand. My hands didn't even look like my own, folded in my lap, hiding inside a new pair of white gloves. "You must be worried about the hospital," Miss Vest said.

I shook my head. "Not too much," I told her. Luckily, my appointment at the army hospital in Washington wasn't until the next day. Dr. Boone had said the doctors would need to break the bone again and then reset it in a cast. But with all the rushing around before the trip, there hadn't been an extra minute to think about what they were planning to do to my arm.

I sat up taller in my seat, and Miss Vest started pointing out the best sights: the U.S. Capitol and a long stretch of park called the Mall, where people sat on benches throwing bread crumbs to fat-chested birds.

"Is that the Washington Monument?" I

gasped, craning my neck so that I could stare higher and higher to its sharp tip-top. I had seen it in the guidebook, looking like a giant exclamation point hanging over the city. I always wanted to use exclamation points in my writing at school, but my words never seemed exciting enough to deserve them. Now I gazed out the taxi window and pictured myself scribbling, "Tall buildings! Fancy stores! Water fountains shooting into the air!"

Then, all at once, the taxi was slowing down. "Look, April," Miss Vest said under her breath. "We're here."

We drove through a set of iron gates, and stretched out in front of us were acres of smooth green grass with the president's mansion sitting right in the middle like a big frosted birthday cake. Now I understood why people called it the White House. It was so dazzling white, it made my eyes water just to look at it.

A swarm of butterflies fluttered up into my throat and my hands started to sweat inside my gloves. The taxi was pulling to a stop under a stone arch and a guard was hurrying out to open the car door for us and pay the driver for our ride.

"Here we go," Miss Vest whispered, and I slid across the seat and stepped out after her, trying to smooth down the wrinkles on the back of my dress.

An old man who called himself the chief usher and wore a tie knotted tight around his wrinkly neck was waiting for us inside. He gave a little bow and told us he would be pleased to escort us to meet the first lady. As we followed him down the long quiet hallways, our feet didn't make a sound on the thick carpets. It felt as though we were gliding, as if the rooms to the left and the right would go on forever.

Every once in a while, the chief usher stopped and showed us something new. "The China Room," he said, pointing at glass cases filled with plates and cups and dishes. "You can see the patterns used by former presidents."

We glided along more until we came to a wall of statue-ladies wearing long gowns of satin and silk covered with pearls and sparkly beads. "Favorite gowns worn by first ladies of the past," he announced in his serious voice. Miss Vest nodded. I nodded, too.

Finally he led us up a wide flight of stairs and into a beautiful room with no corners. It was shaped like an oval and filled with light. "Mrs. Hoover will be with you shortly," the usher said and slipped away. Miss Vest and

I sat in chairs that reminded me of the thrones in the storybooks at school.

We waited for what seemed like a long time. I crossed and uncrossed my legs, breathing in the smell of lemon furniture wax and listening to the gold clock on the shelf above the fireplace ticking away.

"I remember how petrified I was the first time I sat in this room," Miss Vest said. "I was here for my interview for the teaching job at the school. It seems like such a long time ago."

I could tell Miss Vest was trying to get me to settle down. I watched her look around the room until her eyes landed on an old painting on the wall. The man in the painting had long fluffy sideburns and a big white fancy bow tied under his chin, and he stared down at us with mean snake-eyes.

Miss Vest stuck out her tongue at him, trying to make me smile. I was just letting out a laugh when Mrs. Hoover breezed in.

"What's so funny?" she asked as we stood to greet her.

"Oh, nothing," Miss Vest said, giving Mrs. Hoover a little hug and sneaking a glance at me. "We're just thrilled to be here."

"Well, there's more to come," Mrs. Hoover said, raising one eyebrow. "Follow me."

She took us back down the staircase to a place she called the State Dining Room. I felt tiny as I stared up at the high ceiling and the huge, jeweled light fixtures hanging down. Mrs. Hoover said the room was mostly used for grand dinners to welcome important visitors from other countries. But for us, they had set a pretty table at one end by a marble fireplace and made it cozy with tall screens and leafy plants in china pots.

We sat down in our places, and I spread the big linen napkin over my lap like Miss Vest had taught me. All of a sudden, I didn't feel brave enough to ask Mrs. Hoover about the park. But I had to find out the truth. I had to think of a way to prove Dewey wrong.

I thought about my question all through lunch, as the waiters set plates of food down in front of us and then swiped them away as soon as we were done. The food was good — thin slices of ham, mashed potatoes, and tiny spring peas — but I could barely taste a thing, with my brain so twisted up in wondering how to bring up the park.

"You're awfully quiet, April," Mrs. Hoover finally said. "Is your arm bothering you?"

"No, ma'am," I said. "It's not hurting me a bit . . . but there's something else I've been wanting to ask you, if you don't mind."

Miss Vest looked up from her piece of lemon pie.

"Yes, dear?" Mrs. Hoover said. "You can ask me anything."

I rubbed at the corners of my mouth to make sure there wasn't a piece of pie crust hanging there.

"Well, I was wondering about Camp Rapidan. People have been talking a lot lately about what they're gonna do around there."

Mrs. Hoover looked confused. "Whatever do you mean, dear? Do what around Camp Rapidan?"

"I mean the — the park. People say the government is planning to change everything. . . . That they're wanting to take our homes . . . clear folks out and put gates around the bottom of the mountain and make a park so visitors can come and see the Blue Ridge."

I waited for Mrs. Hoover to wave her hand at the air and say, "Nonsense!"

But she didn't. She set her fork down on the edge of her plate as quiet as she could, and Miss Vest shifted in her chair. I could feel the hairs along the back of my neck start to prickle up.

"Well, dear," Mrs. Hoover started, "you

know there have been plans to create a national park in the Shenandoah area for a long time — long before the president and I ever began looking for a place to build a summer home. I'm surprised you haven't heard about it before."

I stared, not believing what I was hearing.

"It's true that plans for the park are moving forward little by little," Mrs. Hoover went on, "but you mustn't worry. There's absolutely no reason for you or your family to be alarmed. The men in charge of the effort are doing everything they can to make sure that all the residents in the area will be treated fairly and taken care of, park or no park."

"But what about —"

I turned to Miss Vest. She didn't say anything, but something in her eyes or the tilt of her head told me I better save my questions for later, for when Mrs. Hoover didn't have so many other things to worry about, like the children by the railroad tracks or her husband trying to win another election.

I let my voice trail off. Then, before anyone could try to change the subject, the waiters were back, whisking more plates away and asking us if we'd care for coffee or tea.

Eighteen

Wit came to fetch Miss Vest and me from the train station after our return from Washington. As I stood on the platform, holding my sling against my stomach and trying to hear his voice over the rumble of the train, I started thinking maybe the ether the doctors had given me at the hospital hadn't worn off yet. Two full days had passed since they had put a mask full of the medicine over my face to make me go to sleep while they broke the bone in my arm again. Already my afternoon at the White House and all the finery of our eighth-story hotel room in Washington seemed like a dream.

But now Wit was saying something about Aunt Birdy, something I didn't understand, and for a minute, everything turned dark and fuzzy just the way it had when I breathed in the strange, sweet-smelling gas at the hospital.

Miss Vest spoke for me. "What do you mean, Wit? How sick is she?"

"She's resting pretty well now," Wit said. "But she had us going for a while there. Mr.

Jessup was the one who found her. He happened to stop by to see her the same afternoon you left for Washington, and she was in bed in the middle of the day. We called in Dr. Hunt right away. He says it's pneumonia."

"Pneumonia?" I repeated, scrambling to remember what that word meant.

"It's in her lungs," Wit told us. "She just can't seem to get enough air, and she's got a nasty cough. Dr. Hunt wants to move her to a hospital, but she won't budge, so he's given her some medicine to help clear up the inflammation in her chest."

"Will she be all right?" I asked, my voice coming out in a whisper.

Wit put his arm around me, being careful not to bump my plaster cast. "We'll just have to keep a close eye on her. Mrs. Jessup is watching her while we're gone."

A nasty cough. I had heard it that day when I went to see Aunt Birdy after my trip to Camp Rapidan. It was a dry little hacking sound, but I was in such a rush to get back to the schoolhouse, I barely even noticed. Now I remembered all the signs. She had a fire going and she never got up from her rocker, even though it was a warm spring afternoon.

Poor Aunt Birdy. She was so happy for me

200

when I told her I was headed to Washington, D.C., even when she must have been feeling sick. But I had brushed off her slew of questions just like I was brushing off a fly.

Wit reached for our suitcases.

"Does Mama know?" I made myself ask.

He shook his head. "I went out to tell her, April, but nobody was home. I finally just slid a note under the door."

My voice came out sounding sharper than I meant. "That wouldn't do any good. She can't read."

"Oh," Wit said. He looked embarrassed.

"Well, let's not worry about that now," Miss Vest said, grabbing my hand. "Let's go tell Aunt Birdy we're home."

I half expected Mama to be there when I opened Aunt Birdy's door, but it was only Mrs. Jessup. I didn't like seeing her wedged in Aunt Birdy's rocker, sitting among all my grandmother's special keepsakes. When we walked in, she was holding the red cardinal feather, and I could tell things had been moved around on the shelves.

"She's sleeping now," Mrs. Jessup told us. "I heated up some broth a little while ago and managed to get a few swallows down her."

I could see Mrs. Jessup eyeing my cast

and sling. "How was your trip, April?" she asked with a little sniff.

"Just fine," I said. Then I turned to Wit and Miss Vest. "Can I go in and see her now?"

Wit nodded. "We'll be right out here if you need us."

I slowly opened the door to the back bedroom and stepped inside, trying not to let the hinges creak as I shut the door behind me. Aunt Birdy was still sleeping and I tiptoed over and peered down at her, holding my breath so I wouldn't wake her.

I barely recognized the woman in the bed, lit up by the dusty beam of sunlight streaming through a crack in the curtains. She took long raspy breaths and her face looked as shriveled and yellow as a dried apple peel. Her white hair, usually pulled back in a bun, lay across the pillow in dirty strands. But that wasn't what sent a chill running through me. I had never seen Aunt Birdy so still before. . . . Surely I had never seen her sleeping. Ever since I could remember, she was always up at dawn, flitting from one chore to the next without stopping until everyone else had gone home and headed off to bed. The only time she halfway rested was when she sat in her rocker, polishing her stones. Now I kept expecting her to hop up any second and say, "Come on, Apry, the day's a'wasting."

I pulled a stool over to the bed and reached up to touch the tall cherry-wood headboard with my free hand. Grandpap Lockley had made the bed as a wedding present when he and Aunt Birdy were married. For good luck, he had carved special patterns in the fine red wood — circles woven together, with flower petal shapes inside. Aunt Birdy always kept the bed polished and gleaming. It was the prettiest piece of furniture in the whole house, and it stood out like some sort of rare jungle bird next to the bare plank floors and the walls where Aunt Birdy had plastered old newspapers to keep the wind from whistling through the cracks.

Mama once told me that when she was a little girl she believed that if she traced the carvings on the bed with her fingernail every night she could keep bad spirits and haunts away. Didn't do her much good, I thought. Still, for the next five minutes I traced my fingernail along Grandpap Lockley's grooves and notches and curlicues. By the time I finished, I was so worn out with praying for Aunt Birdy and listening to her raggedy breathing, I wanted to crawl into the big bed and go to sleep beside her.

But then Wit and Miss Vest were poking their heads in. Wit had his little black bag so I moved out of the room to give him space. Mrs. Jessup was still sitting in Aunt Birdy's chair. For a while she didn't say anything. She just rocked, every once in a while reaching out to pick up one of Aunt Birdy's stones. Then she said, "Funny how your mama hasn't come over yet. You'd think she'd want to be with Birdy right now."

"Mama doesn't even know she's sick," I told her in a rush. "Wit said she wasn't home when he went to tell her."

Mrs. Jessup kept rocking. "Oh, she knows all right. I sent Dewey down to make sure she got the news. She was out at the pump. Dewey says he told her and she just nodded and went back to pumping."

I could feel the blood rushing to my head. I wanted to scream. I wanted to scream so loud that Mama would hear me all the way over at Doubletop. I wanted to throw myself on Mrs. Jessup and rip Aunt Birdy's stones out of her stubby hands. But I just stood there in the middle of the room, swaying a little, like a dried-up branch in the wind.

Nineteen

The next few days passed in a blur. While Aunt Birdy drifted in and out of sleep, neighbors drifted in and out of the house, bringing more and more food and advice. Thank goodness Wit and Dr. Hunt kept coming round to help me keep the visits short and work my way through all those pots of soup and chicken and dumplings.

Miss Vest came to help as often as she could, too — before and after school and during lunch recess. She worried about me spending so much time at Aunt Birdy's bedside.

"April, how can you keep this up?" she asked me one day during her noon visit. I could feel her studying me as I ladled out a bowl of broth for Aunt Birdy. I made sure to keep my good arm steady and not to spill a drop in front of her.

I shrugged. "I've gotten so used to doing things one-handed I don't even think about it anymore."

"I'm not just talking about your cast," Miss Vest went on. "You've got circles under your eyes. I'm sure you're not getting much rest, sleeping on the floor here." She frowned down at the messy little pallet of old quilts and blankets I had made by the fireplace. I'd never admit it, but Miss Vest was right. I woke up at least five or six times a night, whenever I heard Aunt Birdy's deep, rattling cough or when she tossed and turned, making the springs in her bed creak.

"Dr. Hunt says her lungs are clearing up more every day," I said, trying to sound cheerful.

"That's true. But she's a long way from taking care of herself, and what about all the school you'll be missing? And what about money, April? I know Aunt Birdy has some savings up in that jar in the cupboard, but that money can't last forever." She touched my arm. "I've been thinking. Maybe I should go see your parents again. I'm sure they're not really aware of how sick Aunt Birdy is."

"They know," I said. "The whole mountain knows."

"But maybe Dewey didn't explain the situation to your mother very —"

I plunked a spoon in the bowl so hard that broth went splashing over the sides. "She knows! She just doesn't care!"

I could feel my face turning hot. It was

going on three years that I had known Miss Vest, and I couldn't remember ever raising my voice to her before.

"All right, April," she said quietly. "We'll wait and see."

I nodded. There was nothing left to say. There was no one to take care of my grandmother but me.

I picked up the bowl and Miss Vest followed me through the house to the back bedroom. Aunt Birdy woke up when we came through the door. "Time to eat again already?" she asked in a scratchy whisper.

"That's right," I said. "Let's see if you can eat more than five bites this time." I set the soup on the dresser while Miss Vest fluffed her pillow and helped her to sit up.

Aunt Birdy drew in a ragged breath. "I'll try to eat, honey. I need to get up on my feet soon. Otherwise, I'll turn silly staring at these four walls, trying to figure out what all those old newspapers say."

Miss Vest and I looked around the room at the yellowed papers plastered over the cracks, and laughed. It was the first time Aunt Birdy had sounded like her old self since we had come back from Washington. Plus she had given me a wonderful idea.

I rushed over to the bed and squeezed her hand. "Aunt Birdy, I can help you pass the time by reading to you. And I promise I'll find a lot more exciting things to read than these old newspapers."

Miss Vest's eyes brightened. "That's right, Birdy. April could come to the classroom and pick out books you might like. Then she'd be doing you both a favor. She'll keep you entertained and keep up with her reading at the same time."

A smile flickered across Aunt Birdy's face, and the next day I was rushing off to the schoolhouse to bring back as many books and magazines as I could carry.

Reading saved Aunt Birdy and me that spring. We worked our way along every shelf at the schoolhouse — through a year's worth of *Child Life* magazines, three or four encyclopedias, a stack of McGuffey's Readers, the Holy Bible, *Little Women*, *Grimms' Book of Fairy Tales*, and my favorite, *Black Beauty.*

Aunt Birdy didn't mind when I stuttered over hard words or skipped to something new if a certain fairy tale or magazine article didn't catch my fancy. She closed her eyes and listened and seemed to breathe easier whenever I was reading, stretched out beside her on the big cherry bed. Sometimes I thought she had fallen asleep, but if we got interrupted by Dr. Hunt's visits or one of the neighbors stopping by she always knew exactly where we had left off.

"No, no, Apry," she'd tell me. "We're on Chapter Seven," or she'd say, "You did that part already, honey. Get to the part where Aurora pricks her finger on the spinning wheel."

Pretty soon I started to believe that it wasn't rest or Dr. Hunt's medicines that were curing Aunt Birdy. It was my reading. When the weather was fine, I coaxed her out to the front porch with promises to read poems from *A Child's Garden of Verses.* And sometimes I read straight through mealtimes because Aunt Birdy would be listening so hard, she would keep taking bites of food without even knowing it.

Living in our little world of books, it was easy to forget about life beyond the front porch. My trips to Taggart's for groceries or up to the schoolhouse to fetch more books were my only reminders that life was still carrying on around me.

One afternoon when I was in the classroom, looking through a stack of *National Geographic* magazines, Dewey wandered over to talk to me. I had barely seen him since my trip to Washington.

"How's Aunt Birdy?" he asked.

"She's better. She's taking a nap right now."

"So I never got to ask you, April. How'd you like the White House?"

"I liked it just fine." I was starting to feel suspicious, especially when I saw Dewey check over his shoulder to make sure Miss Vest was still busy across the room.

"So I bet you never did it, did you?" he whispered.

I pretended I didn't know what he meant. "Did what?"

"Ask the Hoovers about the park."

" 'Course I asked them," I said.

"Well . . . what'd they say?"

With all his questions and my struggling to manage the magazines one-handed, I could feel the sweat beading up over my top lip. "Mrs. Hoover said she didn't know what the devil you were talking about," I lied.

Dewey cut his eyes at me, but before he could get any further, I shoved the three best magazines into my bag and headed out the door. I was surprised at myself. After talking to Mrs. Hoover at the White House, I knew there was truth to what Dewey was saying about the park. But the lie had fallen out of my mouth as smooth as syrup. Still, I couldn't worry about that now. I had to get Aunt Birdy well first.

Daddy was in the front room waiting for me when I got back to Aunt Birdy's. I stood in the doorway holding my bag of magazines, gawping at him.

"Hey, April," he said, taking a step closer like he wanted to hug me. But then he stopped short. "How you getting along?"

I didn't answer. A sharp metal taste filled my mouth, and I felt a wave of something black and powerful pushing up inside my chest.

Daddy looked down at his shoes, shaking his head. "I know, April," he said. "I know. It's been so long. . . . But I think I've done right all this time, letting you stay with Miss Vest. I think you been better off with her, going to school and learning so much. I know what a fine student you are. Miss Vest, every so often she sends us your drawings and stories and those test papers of yours with gold stars on them."

I tried to keep my face blank, but I could feel the surprise widening my eyes. Miss Vest never told me she had been sending them my work all this time.

Daddy went on. "I know your Aunt Birdy's been real sick."

I bit down on my lip. Easy, April, I told myself. Keep still.

211

"Where's Mama?" I asked.

Daddy took another step toward me. "I told your mother we should be here helping you and seeing to Aunt Birdy. And she wants to come, April. She knows school's gonna be out soon for the summer and you won't have Miss Vest here helping you once she goes back to Kentucky for her vacation. Your ma wants to —"

I cut Daddy off, letting my words fly out like bullets. "Miss Vest's not going anywhere. She says she's staying right here with me this summer. Tell Mama I don't need her help. Aunt Birdy's getting better every day."

Daddy looked shocked. He had never seen me so angry before. We stared at each other. He needed a haircut. His hair was so long and shaggy in the back it touched his collar. And his eyes had new wrinkles at the corners. For a minute, I felt myself sinking — sinking back into the memory of sitting on his lap, with his big hands on mine, showing me how to hold the reins and guide Old Dean down the trail.

Then all of a sudden Aunt Birdy was calling from the bedroom. "Apry? You there?"

"You better be going," I said, and even though I knew it wasn't true, I added,

212

"Aunt Birdy doesn't want you coming round here."

Daddy reached in his pocket and brought out a crumpled lump of dollar bills. "Here," he said, dropping the money on the table next to a stack of dirty plates. "You might be needing this. If you get in a fix and need more, just let me know."

Then I stepped out of the doorway for him to pass. I was proud of myself. Daddy had come and gone again, and I hadn't cried a single tear.

Twenty

I didn't tell Aunt Birdy about Daddy's visit — even after two weeks in a row of finding an envelope full of dollar bills poking out from under the straw mat on the front porch. Then one morning I looked up from *Aesop's Fables* to find Aunt Birdy staring toward Doubletop with a confounded look on her face.

"I thought she would have come by now," she said softly. "Do you think she knows? I mean, how poorly I been?"

I laid the book on my lap. "I think she does, Aunt Birdy. But she's so stubborn. She'll never change."

Aunt Birdy fixed me with a pleading look. "But *you've* changed, Apry. Maybe you should go try to talk to her again. You've changed enough in the last two years for the both of you."

I shook my head. "She wouldn't listen. It's too late."

The words burned in my throat. I could see Aunt Birdy's blue eyes welling up with tears, but I still couldn't make myself tell her about Daddy's coming and Mama's offer of help. I couldn't let them back in our lives so easy. For almost two years they had given up on me. Two years!

Besides, it was like I told Daddy. I didn't need their help. Just as she promised, Miss Vest called off her trip home to Kentucky that summer. Every morning she came down the hill to check on us, bringing some sort of treat — a couple of Florida tangerines, a new ladies' magazine, or a packet of Mile High sunflower seeds to lighten up our long days. With Aunt Birdy watching and giving directions from her chair in the shade, Miss Vest and I tended her vegetable garden and pulled weeds around the porch where the snowball bushes and hollyhocks grew.

Wit helped, too. He had a lot more time on his hands now with Camp Rapidan being so quiet for the summer. Miss Vest said the president was too busy fighting the Depression to spend many weekends in the Blue Ridge. And when the Hoovers did come, Wit told us, they weren't bringing as many guests as usual. The president needed a chance to rest and think about something besides banks and businesses and farms going bust.

At first I was unhappy about Wit

spending so much time with us. I saw the way Miss Vest's face turned pink whenever she heard his shoes clumping up the porch steps or how Wit held her hand under the table when he thought no one was looking. But I couldn't stay mad at him for long. Wit teased Aunt Birdy and made her smile, and on top of that, we needed him. He put new shingles on the roof of the springhouse that summer, shoveled thirty years of old manure out of the storage shed, and built a sturdy chicken-wire fence around the garden to keep out the rabbits and the deer.

Near the end of the summer, Wit showed up with a pair of clippers and said it was time to take my cast off. In five minutes, he had cut the plaster down the middle and cracked it back to bare my arm underneath.

"Yuk," I said. My arm looked as brown and shriveled as one of the old wisteria vines growing up the porch railing. Miss Vest ran to get a washrag and a basin of soap and water.

"See?" she said when she had finished. "Looks better already." I tested my arm, bending and flexing it back and forth. It felt light as a reed without the clumsy cast wrapped around it.

"Now, Miss Vest," Aunt Birdy said from her rocker. "You and Wit need to help me talk this girl into going back to school. She's got no business sitting in this dark place with an old lady all fall."

Aunt Birdy didn't talk me into leaving her side until October, when Miss Vest and Wit took the whole class down to the Madison County Fair for the day. The Hoovers had sent money for admission and tickets, and as soon as Aunt Birdy heard about the trip she started pestering me to go along. So the morning of the fair, I found myself climbing into the back of a marine truck piled high with kids and sweet-smelling hay.

It was a perfect fall day, with the maples so red they looked like they had caught fire against the bright blue sky. Wit and Miss Vest drove our truck with one load of kids, and Mr. Jessup and Sergeant Jordan took another load. As we rocked and swayed down the mountainside, all the kids laughed and whooped at every pothole and horse-shoe turn.

I didn't feel much like joining in. For the past week Aunt Birdy had been taking at least an hour longer to climb out of bed in the mornings, and I had noticed her biting her lip whenever she pushed herself up from her chair. "My joints are just a little stiff with the cold weather coming on, that's all," she told me. "You go on to the fair now and have a good time."

Mrs. Jessup and Little Elton had come over that morning to keep an eye on Aunt Birdy while I was gone. I knew Mrs. Jessup would probably wear her out with all her gossip and prying ways. But by the time we hit the open stretch of highway down in the valley, I started to feel the knots in my stomach work loose.

"Hey!" Vernon Woodard yelled. "Do this! It feels like you're flying!" He was kneeling in the hay facing the wind with his eyes closed, his head flung back, and his arms spread wide. At first I ignored him, but when the other kids started flapping and hollering, I couldn't help myself. I stretched out my arms, and the cool rush of wind lifted my jacket and whipped back my hair. It *did* feel like flying, like I was flying far away from long afternoons filled with worrying and chores and too much quiet.

Then Dewey and Alvin and the Woodard brothers started shouting hello to folks we passed on the roadside. We waved at everybody — an old woman pushing a wheelbarrow full of potatoes, a little boy with a fishing pole, even cows grazing in a bean field and a sad-eyed coon dog that watched us from a rickety porch.

At the entrance to the fairgrounds, a sheriff stood directing people where to park in an open field. We hooted and waved at him, too, and I turned just in time to catch Miss Vest staring at me through the back window of the truck. She was smiling, but she looked surprised.

I knew I wasn't acting like myself, but I couldn't help it. I was free. I jumped down from the truck with hay still in my hair and pushed and skipped with the other kids toward the tinkly music and rows of tents. Already there were crowds of people at the fair — men wearing flashy ties and women in dresses and Sunday hats.

"We'll start at the carousel," Miss Vest called out as she led us along. "Let's stand over here while Wit buys our tickets."

The carousel was a sight to behold, with its pointed roof decorated in jewels and mirrors, and bucking horses charging round and round. Once Wit had passed out the tickets, the boys ran for the black stallions with wild manes, while the girls raced around trying to find the mares with the fanciest saddles or the prettiest eyes. Even Mr.

Jessup took a ticket for the carousel. "You think it's a sin to ride that thing?" I heard him ask Miss Vest.

"No, I think it's good, clean, wholesome fun," she said. In the next minute, Mr. Jessup was sitting on a stallion next to me, staring up at the greasy gears and axles that cranked the horses up and down.

After the carousel, we moved on to the tents full of prize-winning jams and pies and quilts. There were huge blue-ribbon hogs and rows of dairy cows and roosters with gaudy feathers. Then Wit and Sergeant Jordan led us over to a dusty corral, where cowboys in big-brim hats and pointy boots were showing off rope-slinging tricks.

It wasn't until the late afternoon, after we had worked our way through the dart-throwing and ringtoss games and a fried-chicken plate lunch and Cracker Jacks, that I remembered the medicine I wanted to buy for Aunt Birdy. I still had money left over from one of Daddy's envelopes, and Mrs. Jessup had told me that at the fair they sold the best cure for rheumatism you could find. So while everyone else played another round of games, I hurried off to find Dr. Minthorne's Miracle Liniment.

After spending most of the day at the fair, I was sure I knew my way up and down the dusty rows of booths. But with dusk falling and the twinkling lights strung between the tents coming on, things looked different.

I stopped at a stall where a man was selling brooms. "Excuse me," I said. "Do you know where I can find Dr. Minthorne's Miracle Liniment?"

The man shook his head. "Never heard of it. But they're selling some other remedies down the way." He jerked his thumb toward a dark line of walnut trees at the edge of the fairgrounds.

I was starting to feel jittery about getting lost and leaving Aunt Birdy for so long, but I wanted to bring her something. I couldn't come home with nothing but a red balloon and a pack of chewing gum to show for my day down in the valley, so I headed in the direction the broom man had pointed.

As soon as I reached the shadowy place under the walnut trees, I knew I had come too far. Some shifty-eyed older boys were standing in a circle, passing around a bottle in a paper bag, and the old woman who was selling home remedies from the back of a wagon didn't even look up when I stopped to inspect her grubby jars full of roots and salves. She just kept grumbling to herself, pawing through an old burlap sack for something she had lost.

I was ready to head back toward Miss Vest and the other kids when one of the boys broke away from the circle and came strolling in my direction. Even though he was about half a foot taller than when I had seen him last, I recognized him right off. It was Poke McClure.

"Hey, ain't that ghost girl?" he called. "Remember me, ghost girl? It's old Poke. Remember? The one who broke your arm?" He stopped, looking me up and down, then let out a chuckle. "Well, would you look at that? I almost wouldn'ta knowed you. Least you got some meat on your bones now. Don't look half bad."

He took a step closer — close enough so I could smell his hair tonic and the liquor on his breath. I glanced around. The old woman was still rooting through her bag, and Poke's friends were starting to wander over.

"What you doin' way down here in the valley? I thought you'd be up on the mountain, setting under that old dead chestnut tree." He glanced around and saw his friends coming. Then he snickered again and started talking louder so they could hear. "Ya learn to read yet, ghost girl?"

I didn't answer. I turned and ran. I could hear Poke bust out laughing behind me.

"Aw, look at that," one of his friends yelled. "You scared her so bad, she let loose of her balloon."

I ducked down a dark pathway between two tents, then scooted along a shed and a row of parked farm tractors. Maybe I was imagining things, but I kept hearing laughing — a low, mocking laugh drifting out from the dark corners behind me. I ran faster, expecting Poke to step out from the shadows at any second, and knowing that every step was taking me farther away from Miss Vest. But then I spotted a crowd of folks up ahead and I almost shouted with relief.

I hurried toward them and squeezed in, trying to put a few bodies between me and the shadows behind me. It wasn't until I had caught my breath that I looked up and realized what everyone was staring at. There was a man standing on the tailgate of a truck, shouting at the crowd. With his wind-burned skin and his thick, knobby hands, he looked like a simple farmer — not the type who was used to giving speeches, but he was so burning mad, the veins in his neck bulged and he was hammering his fist against his leg.

"Do we plan on letting them get away with it?" he yelled. "Letting them take away our land just so some citified tourists can come spread out a picnic where our homeplace used to sit?"

"No, sir!" a woman next to me hollered back.

"And what about Herbert Hoover?" the man went on. "He comes up here, fishing in our creeks, bringing all them marines and building his houses and roads anywhere he damn well pleases. I heard him myself, couple years back, on these same fairgrounds claiming he cared about the people of Madison County. You heard him, too, didn't you?"

People all around me were nodding. I felt my heart start to thump again, like I had never stopped running.

The man was settling into his speech now, feeling more sure of himself. He hitched up his trousers and smiled around at the folks gazing up at him. "Well, it's kind of convenient, don't you think?" he said, leaving his thumbs hooked in his belt loops. "Old Hoover gets to have his fishing camp up on the Rapidan while he sets back and watches us get shoved off our land. And I don't know if you all heard yet or not, but it turns out the living ain't the only ones gonna be evicted to make room for this here park. They're gonna empty out the dead folks, too!"

Everybody fell quiet. "You heard me right," he went on. "Just the other day I find out they're gonna be moving all our grave-yards down to the lowlands. My poor daddy buried up at Thornton Gap, and his daddy, they're all gonna be dug up."

For a minute I forgot where I was. I turned to the woman beside me. "That's not right!" I cried, forgetting to keep my voice down. "My brother's buried up near Big Meadows and I know the Hoovers. They'd never let that happen. Mrs. Hoover says they're gonna make sure —"

I stopped. The woman was eyeing me like I was addled.

Then she turned away to listen to the man on the truck. He was shouting again. "Well, now's our chance to let old Hoover know what we think about how he's been treating us," he cried. "We'll just show him next month in the voting booth!"

I couldn't listen anymore. As I turned and worked my way back through the circle of people, I could feel tears brimming up behind my eyes. There was no denying it. The park was coming. But if President Hoover lost the election, who would take care of us then? Franklin Roosevelt prob-ably wouldn't care one bit about the school and all the families living around it. What would happen to Aunt Birdy and to me if the Hoovers went away and the park came in?

Dewey was standing at the edge of the crowd. I shoved past him, heading in the direction that seemed to make the most sense.

"Hey, wait a minute," he yelled as he tagged along after me. "Wait!"

When I didn't stop, he grabbed my elbow. I whipped around just in time to catch him smirking at me with that know-it-all smile of his.

"What do you want?" I snapped. "Fine, I'll say it. You were right about the park all along. You were right!"

Dewey looked confused. "What are you talking about?" he asked. "I was just gonna tell you that you're going the wrong way. Miss Vest sent me out to find you. She says we're heading home soon."

"Oh."

"The rest of the kids are clear over at the outdoor stage," Dewey told me. "Come on."

I followed him past a cotton candy and a fried doughnut stall, not saying a word. The fair had lost its magic for me now. My stomach pitched at the thick smell of frying lard, and the games and booths that had looked so colorful and lively an hour ago now looked rickety and cheap. Plus I still hadn't found the liniment for Aunt Birdy.

But Dewey wouldn't let me keep quiet for long. "What were you carrying on about back there?" he asked. "About the park."

I shrugged, all of a sudden feeling tired to the bone. "That man up on the truck — he says they're gonna do it," I told Dewey. "They're gonna move us out first chance they get."

Dewey slowed down. He scratched his hand through his thick black hair. "Did he say where we're supposed to go once they move us out?" he asked.

"Nope. I don't think he knows. I don't think anybody knows."

Dewey cussed under his breath.

"Why are you acting so surprised?" I asked. "I thought you knew all about it."

"Guess I didn't rightly believe it myself till now."

He shuffled on ahead of me, and soon we came to the wide plank stage. I could see all the kids from school squeezed into the front two rows of seats, gawking up at three fiddlers who were tuning their instruments getting ready to play. Their faces glowed in the bright yellow light from the stage.

"Where's Miss Vest?" I asked.

"She's over there," Dewey said, jerking his head toward the carousel. "Still setting with Wit."

I stood on my tiptoes trying to see around the people passing by. Wit and Miss Vest were the only ones on the carousel, tucked into one of the high-backed painted benches between the horses.

I made a sour face. "What are they doing? The carousel's not even moving."

Dewey nodded. "Yeah. Gears locked up. The fella who runs it, he's trying to fix it. But the thing ain't budged an inch for the last hour or so . . . and Miss Vest and Wit, they ain't budged, neither."

He leaned toward me like somebody else might be listening. "They're fixing to get married, you know."

Just like that, Dewey blurted it out, just like it was nothing. He might as well have been telling me about the weather or a rock in his shoe.

"Yeah," he went on. "Daddy heard 'em talking one night when he was in the coatroom before his lesson. He heard 'em talking about where they're gonna live after they get married. But don't tell nobody. They think it's a secret. You won't tell nobody, will you?"

I shook my head no. The fiddle music had started. It cut through the air so sharp and sudden, I could barely hear Dewey saying, "You all right, April? You all right?"

Twenty-One

When we got home from the fair, Miss Vest still never said a word about marrying Wit and moving away. The longer she kept quiet, the more I could feel something inside me withering, turning curled and brown, just like the leaves on the trees down the mountainside. By November, the skies had gone as gray and cold as stone, and I could feel our house filling up with the same stony silence.

Miss Vest just assumed my worrying over Aunt Birdy was the thing that was holding my tongue — and she was partly right. As if things weren't bad enough, Aunt Birdy's cough was back. Sometimes she coughed so hard I thought her tiny sparrow bones might break into pieces. I kept catching her squeezing her eyes shut, like a wave of pain was passing through her — something worse than her old spells of rheumatism. And worst of all, her eyes barely sparked up now when I stretched out on her bed to read her a new book. But she still wouldn't hear any mention of going to the hospital. When

Dr. Hunt and Miss Vest brought up the idea, she shook her head with a wisp of a smile and said, "You two must want to finish me off with that kind of talk."

Even though I was such sorry company, Miss Vest never quit coming to sit with me in the afternoons once school let out. While Aunt Birdy rested in the bedroom, Miss Vest tried to distract me with tricky arithmetic problems and writing assignments or funny stories about the kids at school. I listened with dull eyes. I was tempted to make fun of her, to smirk at her high, silly laugh and the way she threw her hands around while she talked. But I clenched all my bitterness back behind my teeth, and after a while it got to be kind of like a game — to see how long I could last without yelling, *"How could you do it? How could you be planning to go off and leave us like this?"*

Then one afternoon, without warning, Miss Vest was the one who turned silent. She came in the door, checked on Aunt Birdy, then sat down by the fire and started to grade papers, barely even flicking a glance in my direction for the next hour or so. I kept myself busy cutting photographs out of *National Geographic*s to liven up the walls around Aunt Birdy's bed. It was so still in the front room, you could hear the snip of my scissors as I cut out pictures of the Great Wall of China, of giant red kangaroos in Australia, and of a circle of Indians dancing out on a desert somewhere. I kept sneaking looks at Miss Vest. Her lips were pressed thin, and she was holding her red pen so tight her knuckles had turned white. Maybe she was finally fed up with me and all my peevishness.

I was grateful when a knock came at the door. Miss Vest jumped at the sound, and I pushed the magazines off my lap and hurried to see who it was. I was surprised to find Mr. Jessup and Dewey standing in the doorway. Mr. Jessup had a pained look on his face.

"Hello, April," he said. "Miss Vest here?"

I stepped aside and let them in. "It's over, Miss Vest," Mr. Jessup said, walking up to her and dropping a newspaper in her lap. "Sergeant Jordan just brought the evenin' paper up to the schoolhouse."

At first I had no notion of what they were talking about. Dewey watched me from near the door with his hands shoved in his pockets. Then I peeked over Miss Vest's shoulder and saw the big headlines and Franklin D. Roosevelt's picture spread across the front page. And the truth shot through me like an electric current, leaving me numb. It was November 9, the day after the election, and President Hoover had lost. Lost in a landslide to Roosevelt while I sat hidden away at Aunt Birdy's.

Miss Vest closed her eyes. "The poor president," she whispered. "Poor Mrs. Hoover. . . . They'll be so heartbroken."

Dewey spoke up from the doorway. "What's gonna happen to the school, Miss Vest? Will it close down?"

"Of course not, Dewey," she said quietly. "The Hoovers have paid to run the school so far, but I'm sure Madison County will take over the expenses. Don't worry. The school will be fine."

"Are you sure?"

Everybody looked up at me, surprised.

But now I couldn't stop myself. "What about when you go off and get married?"

Two spots of red flamed up in Miss Vest's cheeks. *"What?"* she asked.

"You're getting married to Wit, aren't you?"

Miss Vest blinked. I could almost see the gears turning inside her head, working to churn out some sort of answer that wasn't a lie but would keep me calm.

I decided to save her the trouble. "You don't have to keep it a secret anymore," I said. "Everybody knows." My voice sounded ugly and mean.

I glanced over at Dewey. He stood frozen, staring like he didn't recognize me.

"April —" Mr. Jessup started.

"No," I said, crossing my arms over my chest. "I want to know when she was gonna tell us. The day before the wedding? The day before she packs up and leaves?"

Miss Vest got to her feet and took a couple steps toward me. "April," she began. "It's true. Wit and I *have* talked about getting married. But nothing's definite yet, and I didn't want to spring this on you with everything else . . . with Aunt Birdy so ill and the election and your mother . . ."

Her voice trailed off.

"So when are you leaving?" I asked flat out.

Her hands fluttered like moths and she wouldn't look me in the eye. "Well, we — we just aren't sure. Now with the Hoovers going out of office, they might need to give up Camp Rapidan. And if that happens, they won't be needing the marines here anymore. And Wit, well, he just doesn't know where he'll be stationed next." She drew in a deep breath. "But April, I —"

That's when I turned my back on her. "I'm going to check on Aunt Birdy," I said.

"April . . . please," Miss Vest begged.

234

I knew better than to look back. All of a sudden, I remembered the first time I ever laid eyes on Miss Vest, the first day she visited the school. I remembered hiding behind the woodpile and seeing her gaze down at the dead chestnut trees. I knew then that she would never stay. And when she looked in my direction that day, I had sprung down the mountainside as fast as I could go, faster than I had ever run before.

"April," Miss Vest said again. She was right behind me and I felt her hand on my arm.

But now I knew better than to turn back.

I opened the door to Aunt Birdy's room and slipped inside. Then I pushed the heavy plank door closed and leaned against it until I heard the sharp click of the latch.

Finally, I heard them leave. I sat in the chair beside Aunt Birdy's bed while the sky outside the window turned from pink to burnt orange to deep blue. When it was almost black outside, I lit the lamp and watched the shadows brush over the dark hollows in Aunt Birdy's cheeks. She slept on and on, and I sat without moving, without reaching out to trace the good luck signs on the headboard or shift my place in the hard-back chair.

I knew it was time to stoke the fires, to heat up the soup and wake Aunt Birdy for supper. But I couldn't seem to rouse myself, and the same thoughts kept running through my head. *They've all left me, Riley and Mama, Miss Vest and the Hoovers, and now Aunt Birdy, and soon they'll take our house too. . . .*

When I looked down again, Aunt Birdy had opened her eyes. She was watching me, studying me almost, like she had been awake for hours. I reached over to squeeze her hand and she squeezed back.

Before I could ask her how she felt, she started talking. "Just now, Apry, you reminded me so much of your mama. You got that same far-off look in your eyes. What were you thinking about?"

Aunt Birdy needed me to be strong. Her voice was so raspy and faint, but just hearing the sound of it made me give in. "I don't want you to leave me, Aunt Birdy," I whispered. "What'll I do? I'll be all alone."

"Oh, honey, you'll never be alone. You got folks who love you so much."

I shook my head back and forth. "Seems like I keep losing them. . . ."

"No, Apry. It's like my stones. Some people, they walk along and just see a rock. They wouldn't see a fish or a moon or anything beautiful. That's got to be practiced, you know, looking deeper. If you just look close enough, you might find something you weren't expecting. You just have to start with a stone. . . ."

I nodded. She was rambling and her eyes were closing again. I gave her shoulder a little shake. "Aunt Birdy, you gotta eat something. You want some supper?"

"No, honey, no," she mumbled, blinking hard, trying to keep awake for me.

"But I made you something special," I told her, hopping to my feet. "It'll only take me a minute."

I had made the potato soup that morning, working from a recipe in one of Miss Vest's ladies' magazines. The recipe called for some things I had never heard of before — dried thyme and golden sherry. But we had onions and potatoes and flour and there was milk and a slab of bacon out in the springhouse. It had felt good to follow the cookbook's instructions one by one and think of nothing else besides chopping and whisking and stirring for a change.

I raced to heat up the fire in the stove, and once the soup was warm, I ladled some into a bowl, grabbed a spoon, and hurried back to Aunt Birdy. But she was asleep again, curled up on her side like a little girl.

"Oh, Aunt Birdy," I moaned. But there was no use waking her. She hadn't eaten much of anything for days. I set the soup bowl on the floor and sat down in the chair beside the bed again to watch and to wait. I don't know how much time had passed before I heard a knock at the door — it was a shy knock at first, then louder.

I knew it was Miss Vest, coming to say she was sorry, to try and smooth things over. But it wouldn't do any good. She was marrying Wit and leaving, and nothing I could say would change that. Aunt Birdy's eyelids flickered, and for once I prayed for her to stay asleep, just until Miss Vest gave up and went away. I grabbed the sides of the chair and held on tight as if a twister was bearing down on me, ready to sweep me away.

It wasn't until a few minutes after the knocking on the door stopped that I looked down and saw my hands clenched in a fist in my lap and remembered Mama. *I was just like her.* Here I was, hiding from the knocking, waiting for Miss Vest to go away, just like Mama and I had all those horrible days after I first broke my arm. Aunt Birdy had even said it — she had said I was the spitting image of Mama, staring out the window with a far-off look in my eyes. *Ghost girl.* I'd never be anything else as long as I kept turning folks away.

I scrambled to my feet and ran for the front door. But by the time I yanked it open, no one was there — just something wrapped in a blanket sitting on the porch, three steps away.

"Wait!" I cried into the icy black night. My voice rang over the mountain and sent puffs of steam into the air. "That you, Miss Vest? Come back! I'm here. *Come back!*" I stared up toward the schoolhouse.

But there was no answer. Only the rattle of dry leaves in the branches, and somewhere down in the hollow a hound barking at the moon.

I fetched the lantern inside the front door, then kneeled down by the strange-looking bundle and pulled the blanket away. My breath caught as I ran my hand along the sharp edges and the smooth wood. I would have known that shape anywhere.

It was the Victrola. And when I looked up to search the dark yard again, Dewey stepped out from the shadows.

"Why?" was all I could say.

He shuffled into the light, then stood kicking his toe against the bottom porch step. "You should have it," he said with his eyes fixed on his feet. "I know you feel like you got nothing left. But the Victrola never really seemed like it belonged to us anyway. You should have it."

"What'd your ma have to say about that?"

"She and Ida weren't too happy, but Daddy thought it was a good idea."

We were quiet for a while as I fingered the stack of records that Dewey had wrapped in the blanket alongside the Victrola. I slipped the top one, "Let Me Call You Sweetheart," to the bottom of the pile, and then hugged the records to my chest. I didn't even care if Dewey saw me weeping.

"Thank you," I finally said.

He shrugged with a little smile twitching over his lips.

I wiped my face against my sleeve. "You think I could ask you for one more favor?"

"What's that?"

"You think you could sit with Aunt Birdy a while? There's something I need to do."

Dewey nodded and followed me inside. I could have kissed him for not asking any questions. He just listened, serious as a preacher, while I listed off instructions: where to sit, where to put the Victrola, what to say if Aunt Birdy woke up. Then I grabbed my coat and the lantern and bolted into the dark.

Twenty-Two

It had been such a long time since I had followed the trail to our place over on Doubletop. But even in the dark, my feet seemed to remember every rut and stone and rise. After a mile or so, I decided I didn't need the lantern anymore. My hands were turning numb holding on to the cold metal handle. And the flickering light threw strange shadows over the bare trees at the edge of the path and sent awful thoughts creeping into my head. What if I had waited too long to fetch Mama? What if Aunt Birdy was gone by the time I got back?

It was easier to think straight in the dark. I hurried down the path, trying to calm myself with good thoughts. Daddy will be there, I chanted in my head, now that he's working on the road so close to home. Daddy will be there to smooth things over between us and convince Mama to come with me.

The chant made me bold — bold enough to run even faster down the trail. I could hear animals scurrying through the brush nearby, and a few times I didn't duck fast enough and low-hanging branches slapped across my face. But I knew if I slowed down, I might turn back. So I never stopped running until I had made it up the sagging front steps of the cabin and banged on the door.

"Mama?" I called. "It's me."

There was no answer. *Daddy must be gone after all,* I thought. Still, I knew she was inside. There were no front windows to peek through, but I could see a sliver of light under the door. And what was that sound? The creak of a chair and the rustle of someone moving. *She was in there.*

"Mama?" I cried again. "Aunt Birdy sent me. She needs you, Mama! She's been calling for you."

I didn't care if I had to lie. I started beating on the door, pounding with my fists. She was in there, hiding, and she wasn't making a single move to let me in, even though her own mother was dying just across the hollow. I had stood by and watched Riley die, but I wasn't planning on letting Aunt Birdy go so easy.

Just then I remembered the back door to the kitchen. It didn't have a lock. For years Mama had been after Daddy to add a latch that she could bolt, but he never seemed to get around to it. I flew down the steps and around the side of the house and it was as easy as taking my next breath. I turned the knob, pushed the door open, and walked through the kitchen.

I felt like I was stepping back in time. Nothing had changed — the same frayed rag rugs and dusty pile of baskets, the same scrubbed kitchen table and splintery floor. And there was Mama, in her chair by the fire with a pile of sewing on her lap. The same sad, worn face and her mouth carved in a hard line.

I didn't give her a chance to look me up and down or say my name. "Why wouldn't you let me in?" I cried. "Why? Didn't you hear me? *Aunt Birdy's dying.*"

Mama bent over her sewing again. "It's too late," I heard her say. Her flat, hollow voice sent chills running along the back of my neck.

"It's not!" I screamed. "She needs to see us together! Just for a minute! I know you can't forgive me, but just give me this one thing and I'll never come near you again. Just come with me now, for Aunt Birdy's sake. Come with me, please!"

Mama didn't look at me. She held tight to her sewing needle, pushing it in and out and in and out of the fabric, and before I knew what I was doing I lunged for the bundle of colorful cloth and ripped it out of her hands.

A look of horror flew over Mama's face. "Give that back," she ordered.

When I didn't move, she reached her hands out like claws and shrieked, "Give that back!" Her face started to crumple. "It's all I got! Give that back!"

I looked down at the cloth in my arms and realized what I was holding. It was a patchwork quilt. I had never seen it before, but it seemed familiar somehow. Then I saw them . . . all through the pattern were pieces from Riley's little Sunday shirt, the one I had saved Mama from cutting such a long time ago. *Riley.* That's all she cared about.

I started to fling the quilt to the floor, then I saw something else. In the far corner of the quilt, worked into the design, was a piece of a doll's dress Mama had made me when I was six. I hadn't seen it for years.

"You kept it," I said with a gasp. I looked up at Mama in amazement. "My doll's dress . . . you *saved* it."

Mama reached for the quilt again, but I took a step backward, cradling it in my arms. "And look. . . . There's my old baby blanket. And there, that's a piece of the apron I used to wear when I helped you with canning."

I sank to the floor, stroking my hands over

the quilt and searching for more patches. It was just like Aunt Birdy had said. If I looked deeper, I might find something I wasn't expecting. *There!* Another one near the middle — a scrap from the blue dress with the lace collar I had worn on the first day of school.

When I lifted my head again, Mama had slumped back in her chair with her hands lying limp in her lap. Tears were rolling down her face.

"Why couldn't you just tell me?" I asked her. "Why couldn't you tell me you were saving my old things, too? That you might use them to make a quilt someday? That's all I would have needed, Mama."

She closed her eyes, but the tears kept dripping down. "I don't know," she whispered, shaking her head back and forth. "I don't know." She kept her eyes closed, even when I laid the quilt over her lap again and left through the front door.

Twenty-Three

Aunt Birdy died that night, but not before she opened her eyes and heard the sweet music from the Victrola filling her home. At first I thought it was the music that lit her face up with such a beautiful glow, but then I heard a noise behind me and turned around to find Mama standing in the bedroom doorway. While the Victrola played, Mama sat with me on the edge of the bed and held Aunt Birdy's hand until she drifted back to sleep.

The next day I asked Mr. Jessup to give the sermon at Aunt Birdy's funeral and without blinking an eye, he said he'd be pleased. I fretted over where to lay Aunt Birdy to rest until Miss Vest promised me that all the talk of moving our cemeteries off the mountain had been just an evil rumor.

"That's sacred ground, April," she told me, hugging me to her chest. "At least that's something that will never change." So we buried her in the little graveyard on the hillside next to Grandpap Lockley, just down the slope from Riley.

Even though it was a funeral, Dewey couldn't help smiling through the whole thing. Mr. Jessup's words were strong and true, and he read one of Aunt Birdy's favorite Psalms from the Bible — number sixty-one. "From the end of the earth will I cry unto thee, when my heart is overwhelmed," Mr. Jessup called out. "Lead me to the rock that is higher than I."

Afterward, all the folks who had loved Aunt Birdy best stood quiet while I placed her favorite stones around the edges of her grave. When everyone had gone, Daddy and I waited as Mama wandered up the hill and stood for a minute, resting her hand on Riley's marker.

By the springtime, Aunt Birdy's stones looked as if they had always been there, hidden among the periwinkle's blue flowers and glossy green leaves. Unless you knew enough to kneel down and peer closer, you would never see that there was a stone shaped like a fish, and others like an egg in a nest, a footprint, or perfect halves of a heart that fit together.

And by the springtime, I was used to living alone in Aunt Birdy's house and going to school without Miss Vest. After Miss Vest's wedding, a new teacher, Miss Lucy

Tuttle, arrived to take her place. Of course, it wasn't the same. Miss Tuttle wore plain blouses and long dark skirts, and she didn't talk with her hands or pay me any special mind. But I had Miss Vest's letters from China to keep her close. She wrote from Wit's military post there, thousands of miles away in a city called Peking.

Every letter was something special. In one, she wrote about dragon parades and rickshaw rides. In another, she described her walks through the dark, narrow streets, where she saw medicine men toting bundles of dried snakes and people called contortionists twisting their bodies into amazing positions. "Our cook is trying to teach me to speak Chinese," she wrote me, "so I can talk with the little children who pull at my skirts in the alleyways."

I counted out money from Aunt Birdy's nest egg to buy writing paper and stamps so I could tell Miss Vest how life was coming along on our mountain. Her letters were always full of questions about Mama and Daddy. "They come to call every so often," I wrote back. "Last week they brought more kindling for the stove. I've invited them to supper next Saturday night. I think I'll make potato soup and fried apple pie for dessert."

"What about Camp Rapidan?" Miss Vest

asked in one of her letters. I hated to tell her the truth — about how President Franklin Roosevelt had come for one visit and decided the trails were too rough to suit him. Now the camp stood empty. When I peeked through the locked gates, I could see wasps making nests in the eaves of the guardhouse and old brown pine needles gathering along the paths.

As the months passed, more and more folks left their homeplaces behind. Nobody knew exactly when the park would open or when we'd all be asked to move. But some people decided to go earlier than they needed to, just so they wouldn't have to see the end. "The Woodards are gone, too," I wrote Miss Vest. "They didn't even say goodbye. I passed by their place yesterday, and all that was left was a skinny tomcat and a pair of dungarees hanging on the line."

As for me, I'm happy to stay put for a while. Maybe there will be more Saturday night suppers with Mama and Daddy. Or maybe Miss Tuttle will offer to lend me one or two of her precious leather-bound books with gold writing on the spine. In the meantime, I'm starting a new collection of stones on the railing. Already, I have a mushroom, a knife, and a lady's dainty slipper. I can't wait for the next fine day. I will sit in Aunt

Birdy's old rocker, polishing until my stones glint like jewels in the sun and dreaming of where I might go from here.

Author's Note

While *Ghost Girl: A Blue Ridge Mountain Story* is a work of fiction, the novel is based on real events and, in some cases, real people, whose lives were forever changed by the opening of the President's Mountain School. The characters of April Sloane, Aunt Birdy, and Dewey Jessup and his family were all inspired by bits and pieces of information that I discovered while reading letters and newspaper articles written about the school and the local mountain people during the early 1930s. Many of the students of the school did, in fact, learn to read with the help of the Sears, Roebuck catalog. And they truly did attend Sunday lessons at the schoolhouse; they held flag-raising ceremonies, ate picnic lunches with Mrs. Hoover in the schoolyard, and each fall made the trip down to the valley to attend the Madison County Fair.

Because Christine Vest, the real-life teacher of the school, left behind such detailed and vivid accounts of her Blue Ridge years in her letters and personal narratives, I felt confident in portraying this little-known heroine and using her actual name. Christine Vest Witcofski returned from Asia in 1936 and spent the following year making a home for her husband and two young sons in one military post after another. In 1938, she made her first trip back to the Blue Ridge, only to find that the families she had once known had scattered. Their cabins stood empty, most waiting to be removed from parkland. Eventually, the schoolhouse itself was dismantled, transported to Big Meadows, and rebuilt as a residence and ranger station.

With the Shenandoah National Park's official opening in 1935, more than 450 families were displaced. Some remained bitter and resisted giving up their homeplaces until the final deadline. Other families viewed their move as an opportunity and were eager to resettle on their own or in one of seven government-built homestead communities in the lowlands, where there was running water and electricity, and better access to schools, medical care, and jobs. A very small list of elderly residents, like Aunt Birdy, were given special status and allowed to live out their lifetime in their beloved homes.

Although this upheaval was painful for

many, there was some comfort for those who had been involved in establishing the President's Mountain School. As Christine Vest Witcofski reflected in 1960:

When [my students] moved from the mountain because of the park, the older ones went to work and the younger ones found their places in the regular schools where they moved. I often wonder what their lot would have been if they had not had all this preparation before leaving their mountain. Because of the school, they were able to take their place in a normal way and many have done very well and have nice homes and fine families of their own today.

After stepping down as president, Herbert Hoover donated the land and buildings of his fishing camp to the Shenandoah National Park. Today visitors can tour the Hoovers' "summer White House" and walk along the rock-lined pathways and beside the trout streams where the president, first lady, and famous guests such as Charles Lindbergh once wandered. The extensive trails throughout the park can also lead hikers back into history. If you decide to venture off a bit, you may find yourself

Students with Lou Henry Hoover on the schoolhouse steps, in 1930. Miss Vest sits at the far left.

standing in the middle of an old mountain cemetery or stumbling upon the stone foundation of an abandoned cabin. And while the exact site of the President's Mountain School has been lost, the Skyline Drive, which winds 105 miles along the crest of the mountains, offers a clear window into the vistas that Miss Vest and her students once admired from the front steps of the schoolhouse. As Christine Vest Witcofski wrote, "In between these mountains lay the valley below. Always some shade of blue, but never the same, any two days of all the years I was there."

About the Author

■■■■■■■■■■■■■■■■■■■■■■■■

Delia Ray is the author of three young adult nonfiction books about American history. She has always been fascinated by old letters. Because of this interest, she was especially thrilled to discover the little-known collection that inspired this novel.

Delia Ray grew up in tidewater Virginia, within a half-day's drive of the Blue Ridge Mountains. She now lives with her family in Iowa City, Iowa.

The employees of Thorndike Press hope you have enjoyed this Large Print book. All our Thorndike and Wheeler Large Print titles are designed for easy reading, and all our books are made to last. Other Thorndike Press Large Print books are available at your library, through selected bookstores, or directly from us.

For information about titles, please call:

(800) 223-1244

or visit our Web site at:

www.thomson.com/thorndike
www.thomson.com/wheeler

To share your comments, please write:

Publisher
Thorndike Press
295 Kennedy Memorial Drive
Waterville, ME   04901